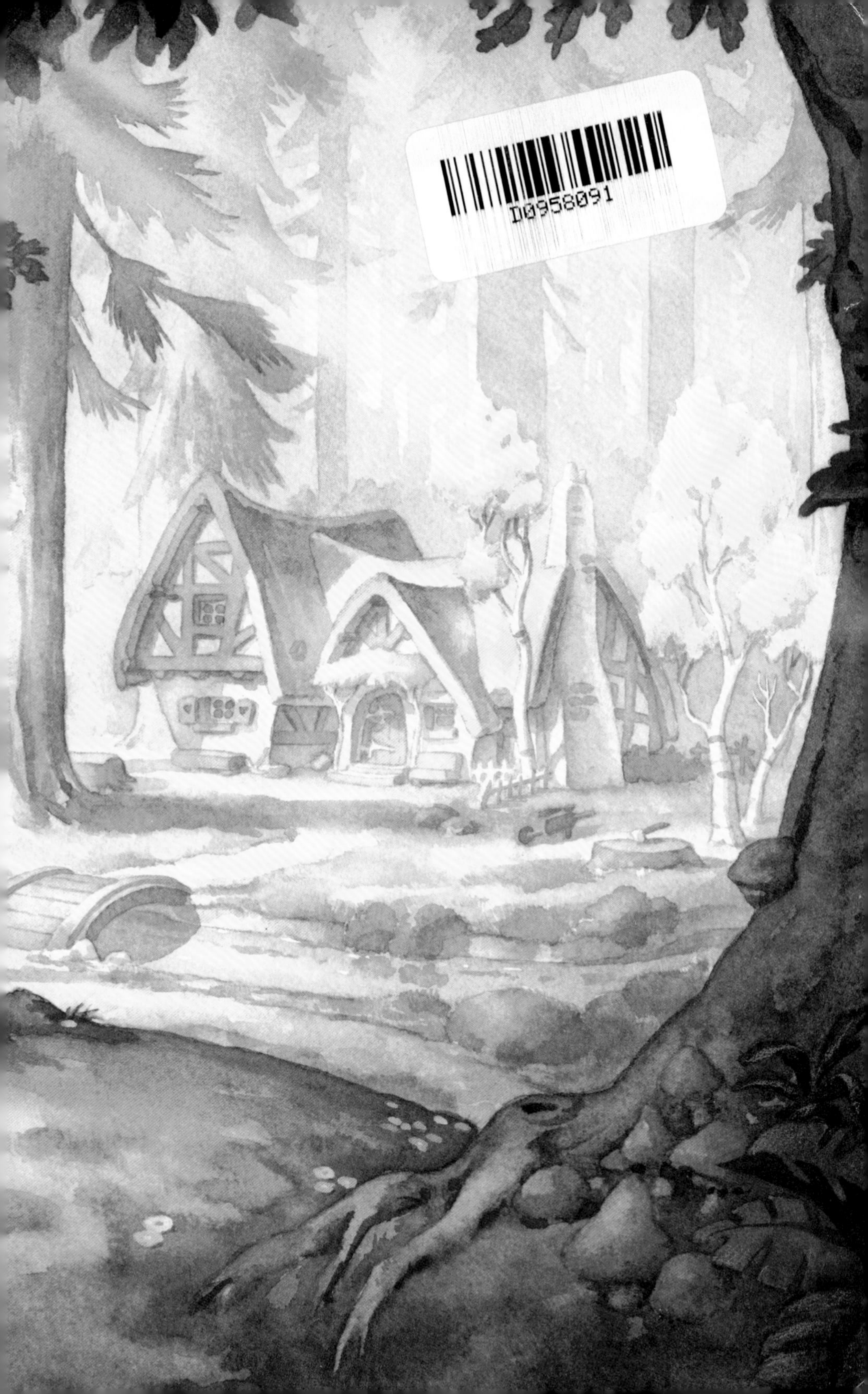

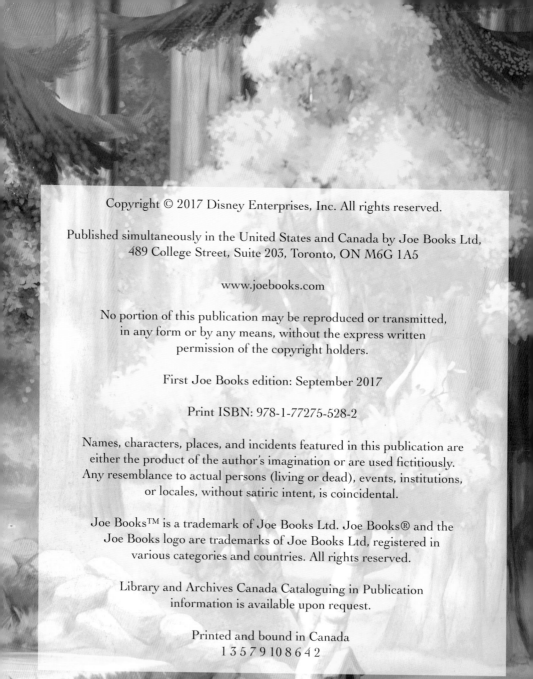

Published simultaneously in the United States and Canada by Joe Books Ltd,
489 College Street, Suite 203, Toronto, ON M6G 1A5

www.joebooks.com

First Joe Books edition: September 2017

Print ISBN: 978-1-77275-528-2

Library and Archives Canada Cataloguing in Publication
information is available upon request.

Printed and bound in Canada
1 3 5 7 9 10 8 6 4 2

Disney

Snow White and the Seven Dwarfs

THE STORY OF THE MOVIE IN COMICS

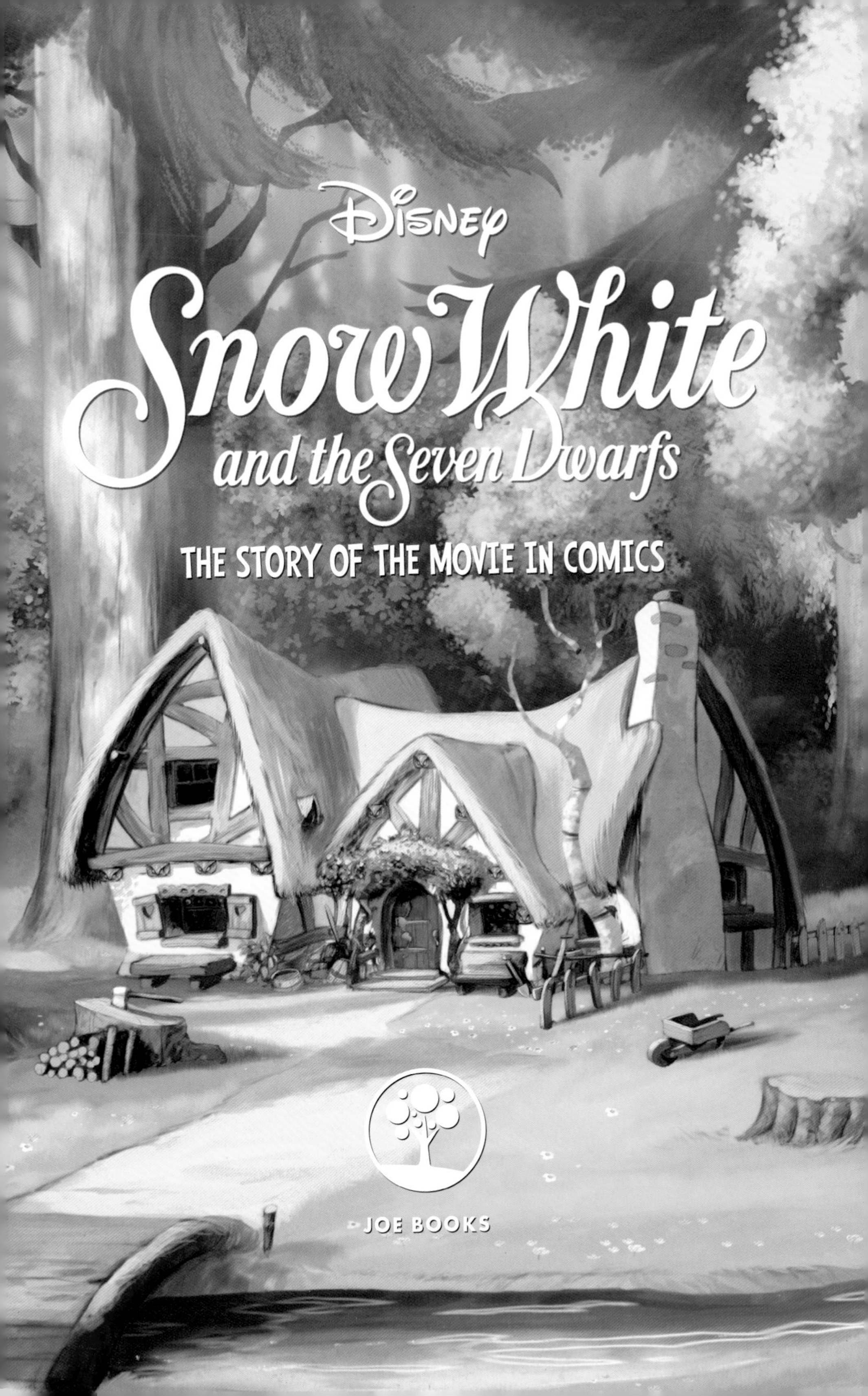

JOE BOOKS

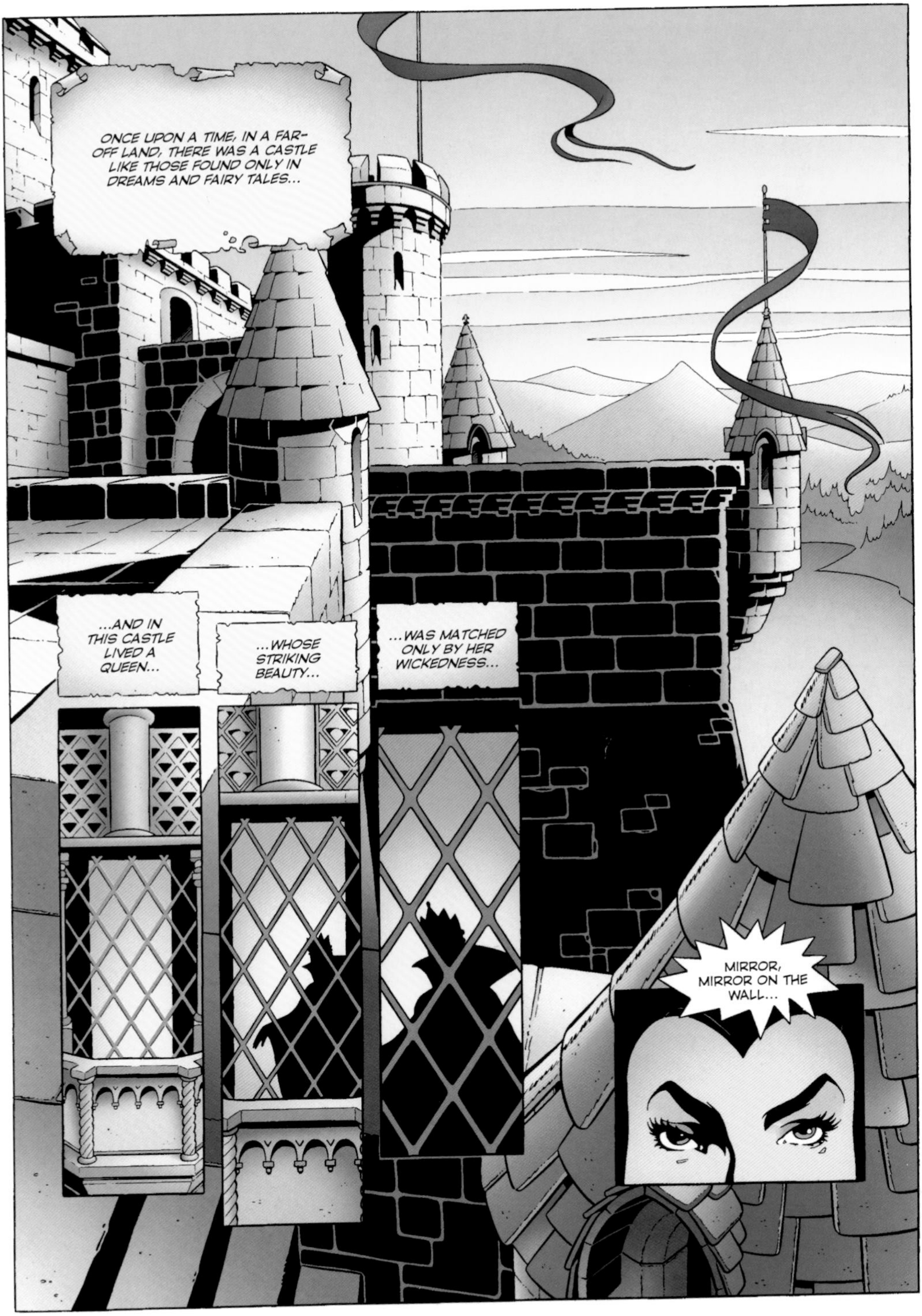
ONCE UPON A TIME, IN A FAR-OFF LAND, THERE WAS A CASTLE LIKE THOSE FOUND ONLY IN DREAMS AND FAIRY TALES...
...AND IN THIS CASTLE LIVED A QUEEN...
...WHOSE STRIKING BEAUTY...
...WAS MATCHED ONLY BY HER WICKEDNESS...
MIRROR, MIRROR ON THE WALL...

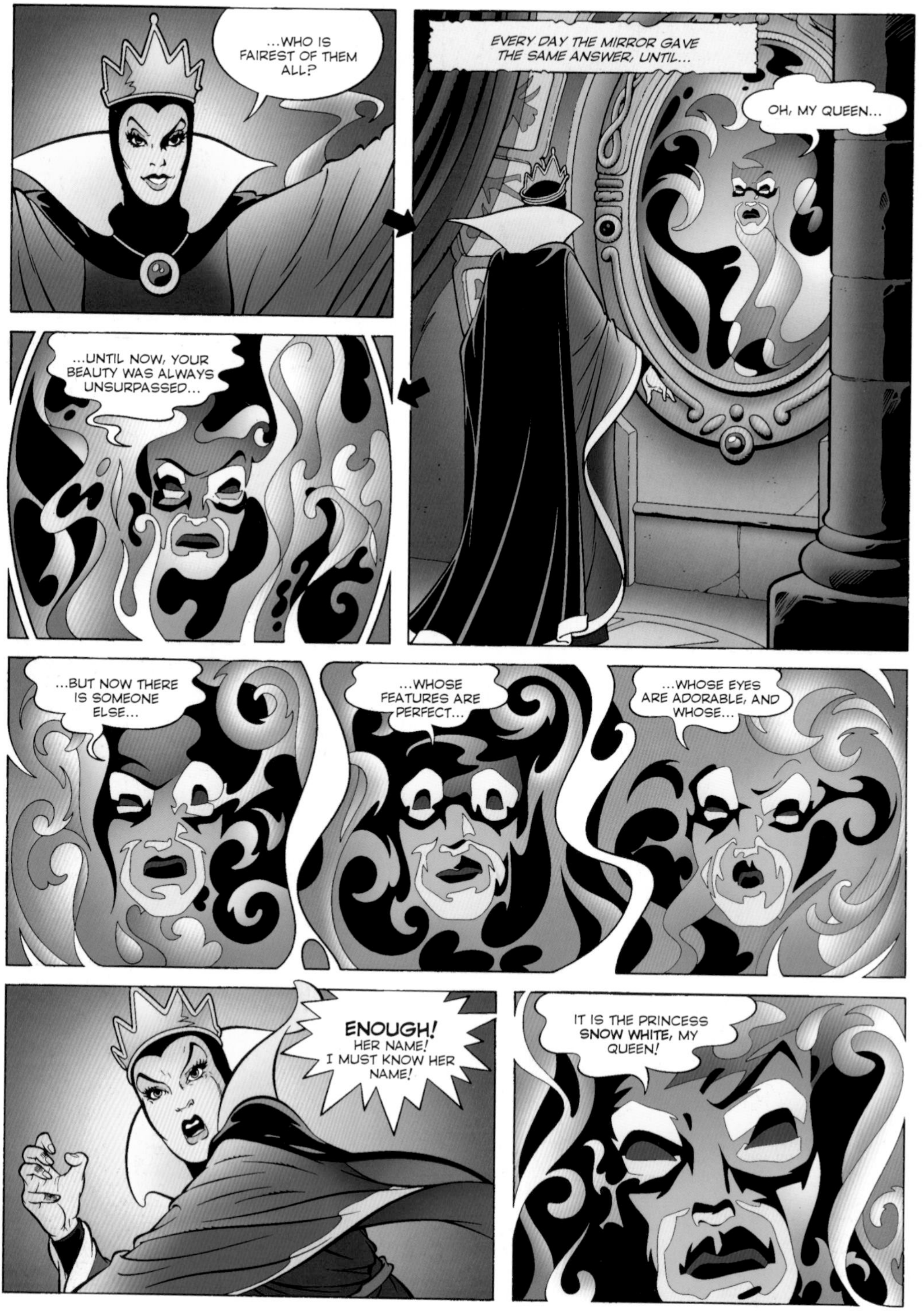
...WHO IS FAIREST OF THEM ALL?
EVERY DAY THE MIRROR GAVE THE SAME ANSWER, UNTIL...
OH, MY QUEEN...
...UNTIL NOW, YOUR BEAUTY WAS ALWAYS UNSURPASSED...
...BUT NOW THERE IS SOMEONE ELSE...
...WHOSE FEATURES ARE PERFECT...
...WHOSE EYES ARE ADORABLE, AND WHOSE...
ENOUGH! HER NAME! I MUST KNOW HER NAME!
IT IS THE PRINCESS SNOW WHITE, MY QUEEN!

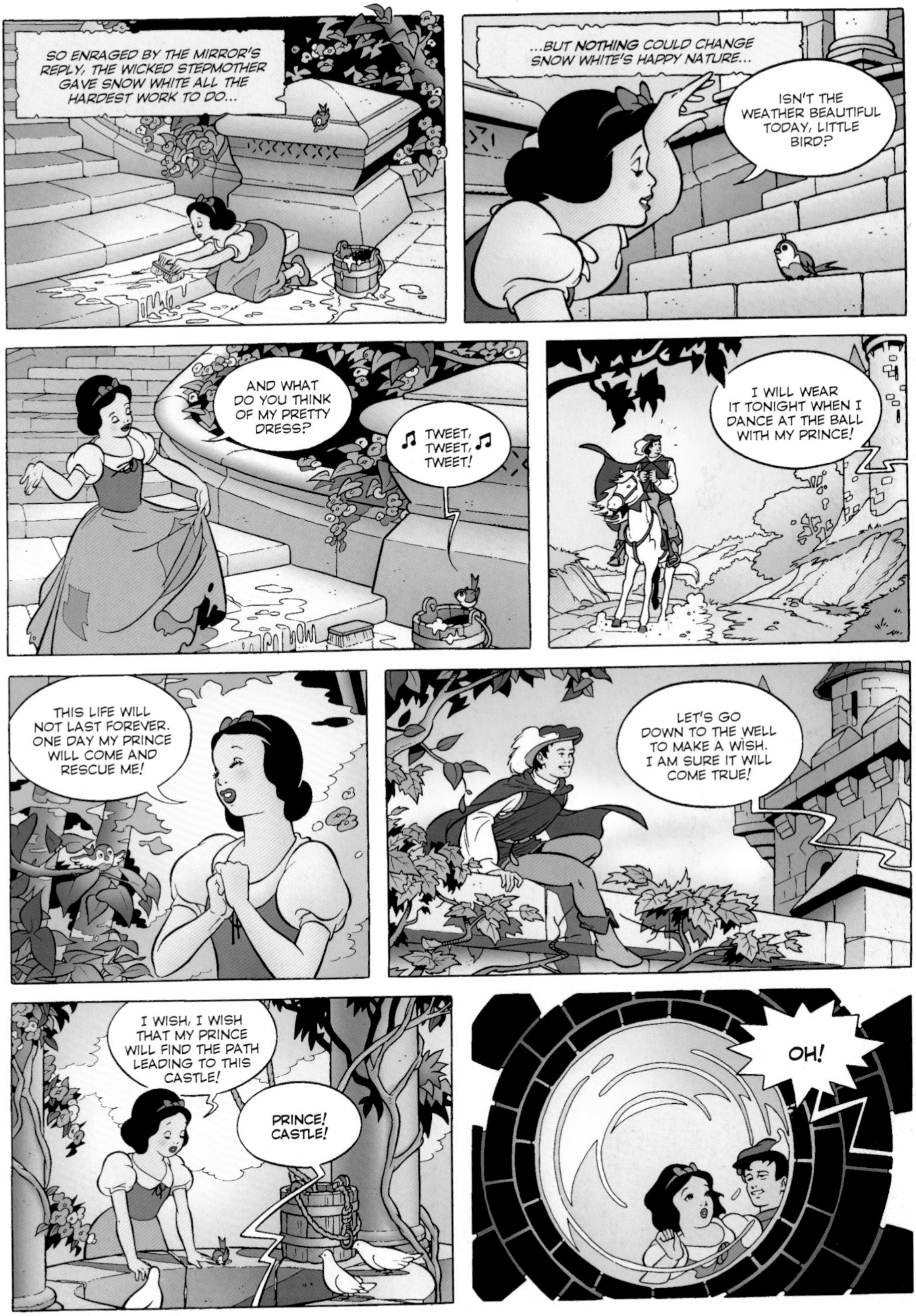
SO ENRAGED BY THE MIRROR'S REPLY, THE WICKED STEPMOTHER GAVE SNOW WHITE ALL THE HARDEST WORK TO DO...
...BUT NOTHING COULD CHANGE SNOW WHITE'S HAPPY NATURE...
ISN'T THE WEATHER BEAUTIFUL TODAY, LITTLE BIRD?
AND WHAT DO YOU THINK OF MY PRETTY DRESS?
♫ TWEET, TWEET, TWEET! ♫
I WILL WEAR IT TONIGHT WHEN I DANCE AT THE BALL WITH MY PRINCE!
THIS LIFE WILL NOT LAST FOREVER. ONE DAY MY PRINCE WILL COME AND RESCUE ME!
LET'S GO DOWN TO THE WELL TO MAKE A WISH. I AM SURE IT WILL COME TRUE!
I WISH, I WISH THAT MY PRINCE WILL FIND THE PATH LEADING TO THIS CASTLE!
PRINCE! CASTLE!
OH!

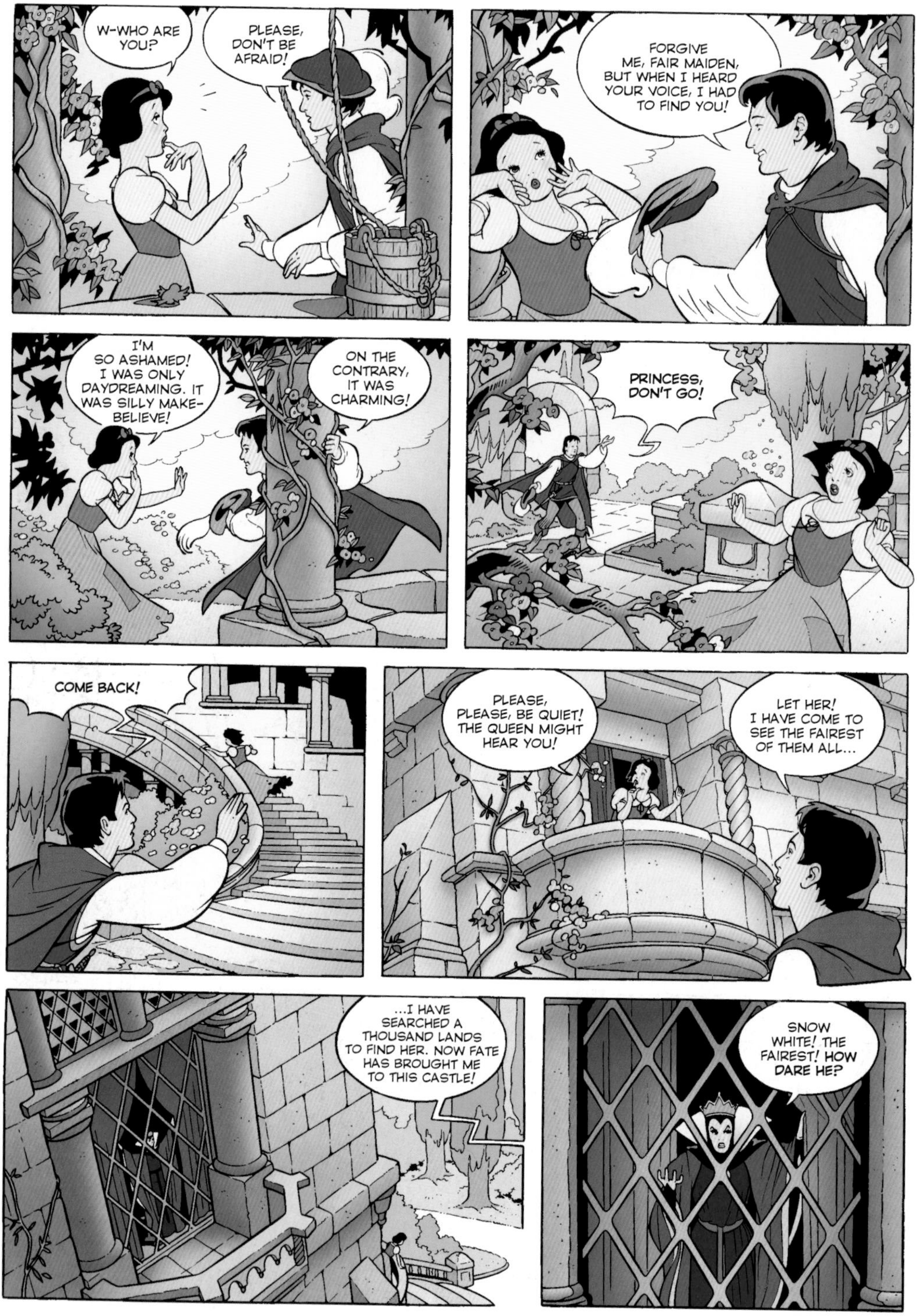
W-WHO ARE YOU?
PLEASE, DON'T BE AFRAID!
FORGIVE ME, FAIR MAIDEN, BUT WHEN I HEARD YOUR VOICE, I HAD TO FIND YOU!
I'M SO ASHAMED! I WAS ONLY DAYDREAMING. IT WAS SILLY MAKE-BELIEVE!
ON THE CONTRARY, IT WAS CHARMING!
PRINCESS, DON'T GO!
COME BACK!
PLEASE, PLEASE, BE QUIET! THE QUEEN MIGHT HEAR YOU!
LET HER! I HAVE COME TO SEE THE FAIREST OF THEM ALL...
...I HAVE SEARCHED A THOUSAND LANDS TO FIND HER. NOW FATE HAS BROUGHT ME TO THIS CASTLE!
SNOW WHITE! THE FAIREST! HOW DARE HE?

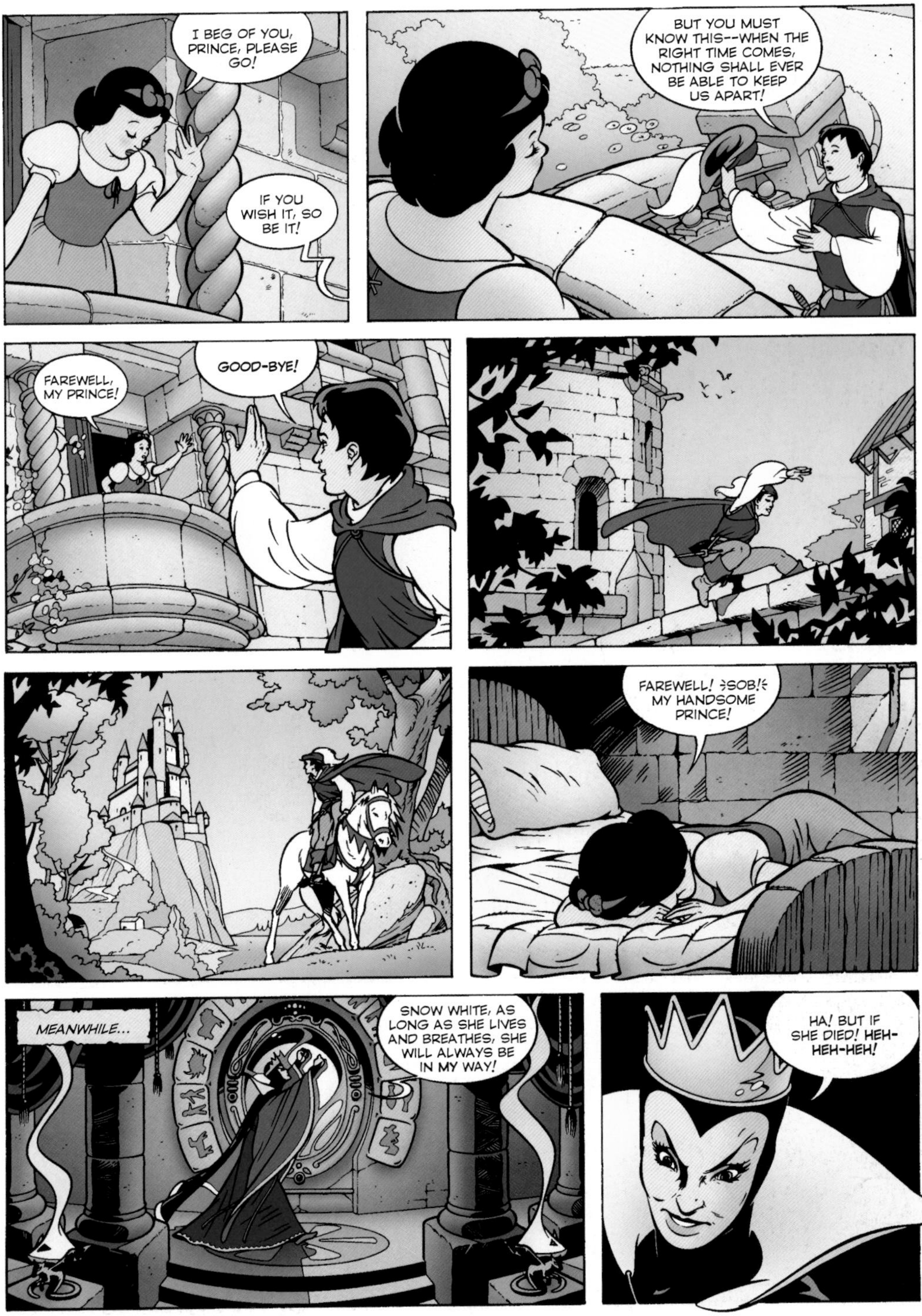
I BEG OF YOU, PRINCE, PLEASE GO!
IF YOU WISH IT, SO BE IT!
BUT YOU MUST KNOW THIS--WHEN THE RIGHT TIME COMES, NOTHING SHALL EVER BE ABLE TO KEEP US APART!
FAREWELL, MY PRINCE!
GOOD-BYE!
FAREWELL! *SOB!* MY HANDSOME PRINCE!
MEANWHILE...
SNOW WHITE, AS LONG AS SHE LIVES AND BREATHES, SHE WILL ALWAYS BE IN MY WAY!
HA! BUT IF SHE DIED! HEH-HEH-HEH!

AND SO, SOON AFTERWARD...

YOU SENT FOR ME, YOUR MAJESTY!

YES! COME IN, HUNTSMAN!

HOW MAY I SERVE YOUR MAJESTY?

I COMMAND YOU TO TAKE SNOW WHITE INTO THE FOREST...

...FIND A DESOLATE CLEARING...

...AND KILL HER!

NO! YOUR MAJESTY, I COULDN'T!

OBEY ME, OR I WILL KILL YOU AND YOUR FAMILY!

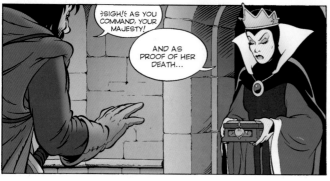

⸮SIGH!⸮ AS YOU COMMAND, YOUR MAJESTY!

AND AS PROOF OF HER DEATH...

...YOU MUST BRING BACK HER HEART TO ME IN THIS BOX!

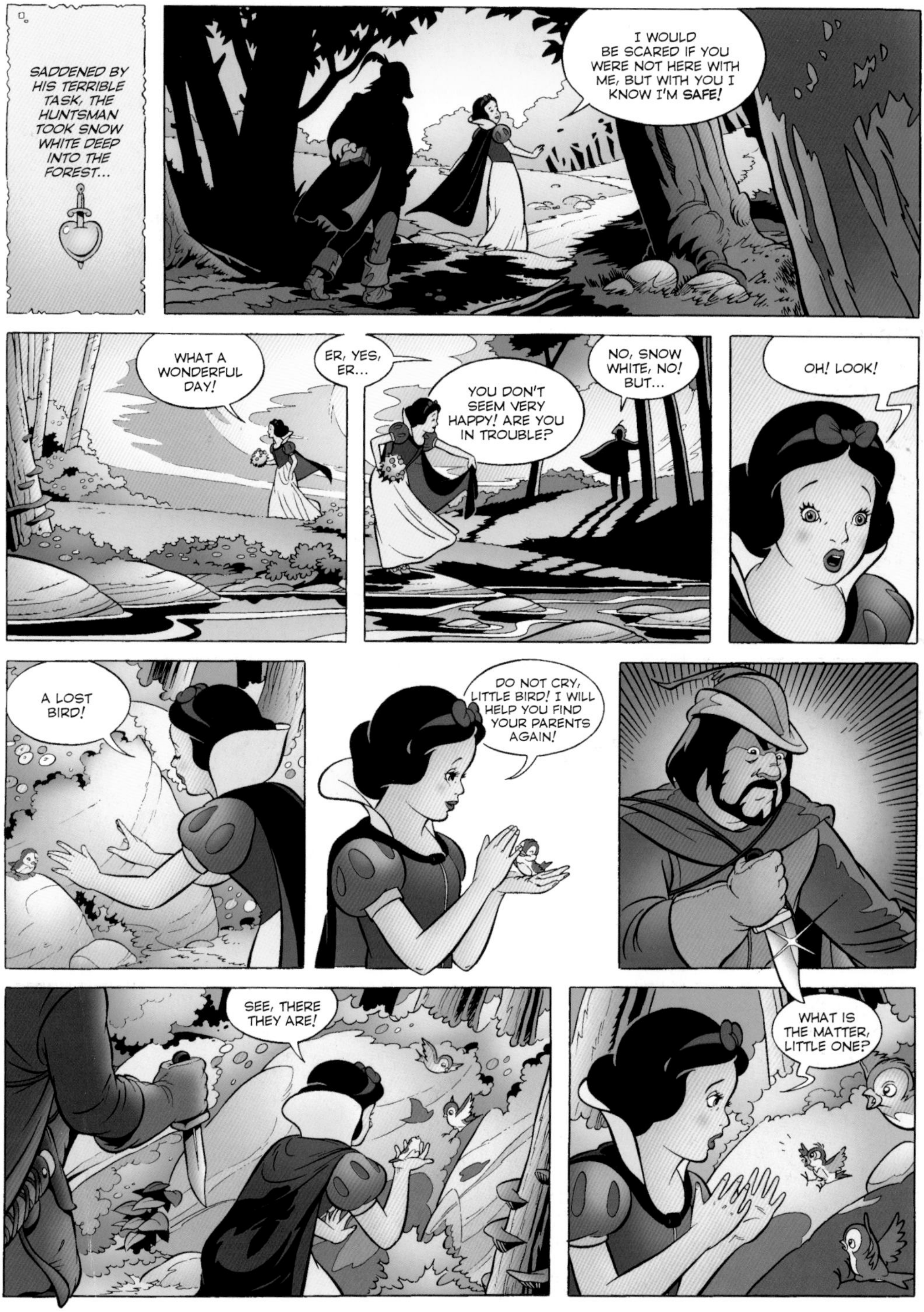
SADDENED BY HIS TERRIBLE TASK, THE HUNTSMAN TOOK SNOW WHITE DEEP INTO THE FOREST...
I WOULD BE SCARED IF YOU WERE NOT HERE WITH ME, BUT WITH YOU I KNOW I'M SAFE!
WHAT A WONDERFUL DAY!
ER, YES, ER...
YOU DON'T SEEM VERY HAPPY! ARE YOU IN TROUBLE?
NO, SNOW WHITE, NO! BUT...
OH! LOOK!
A LOST BIRD!
DO NOT CRY, LITTLE BIRD! I WILL HELP YOU FIND YOUR PARENTS AGAIN!
SEE, THERE THEY ARE!
WHAT IS THE MATTER, LITTLE ONE?

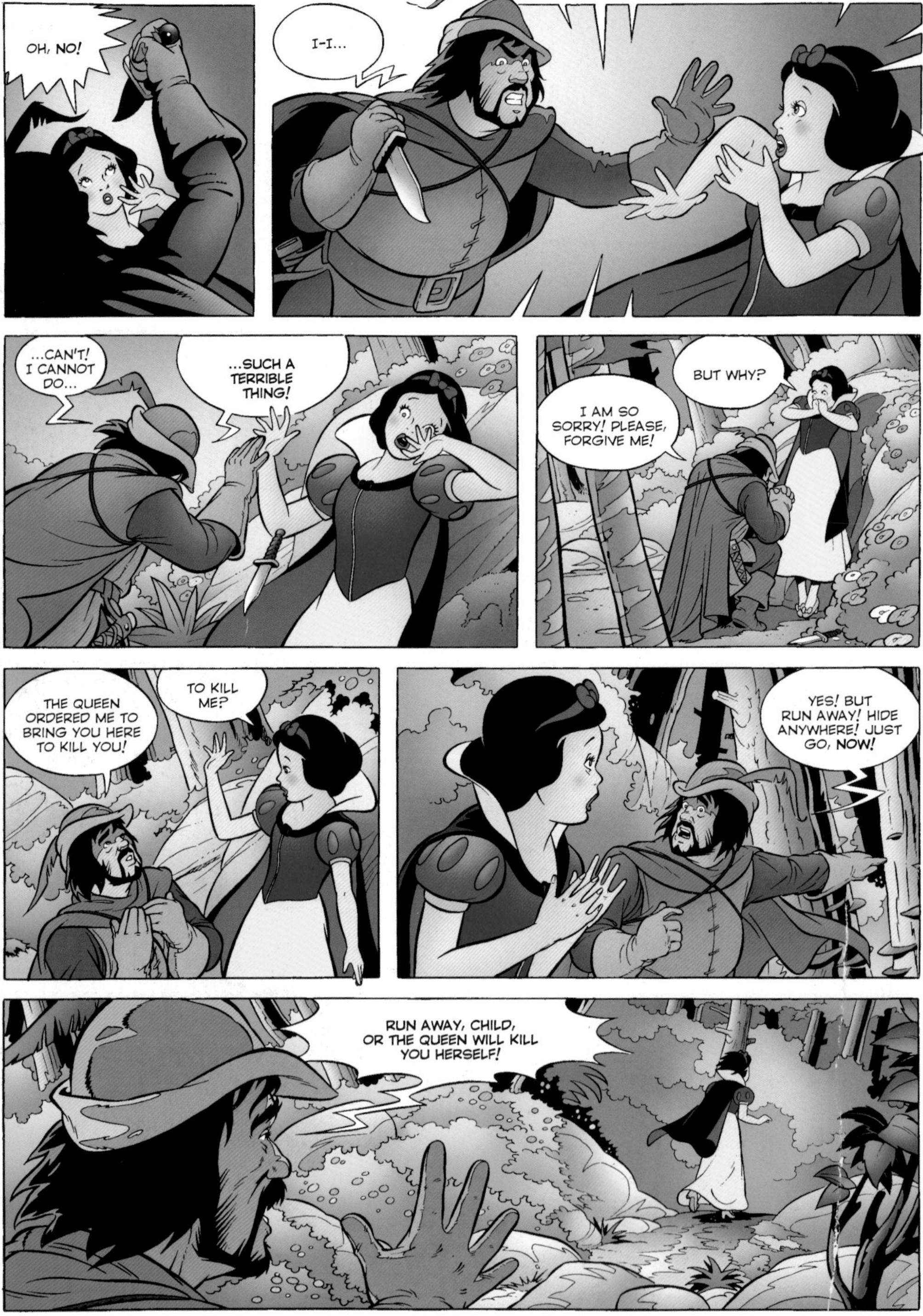
OH, NO!
I-I...
...CAN'T! I CANNOT DO...
...SUCH A TERRIBLE THING!
BUT WHY?
I AM SO SORRY! PLEASE, FORGIVE ME!
THE QUEEN ORDERED ME TO BRING YOU HERE TO KILL YOU!
TO KILL ME?
YES! BUT RUN AWAY! HIDE ANYWHERE! JUST GO, NOW!
RUN AWAY, CHILD, OR THE QUEEN WILL KILL YOU HERSELF!

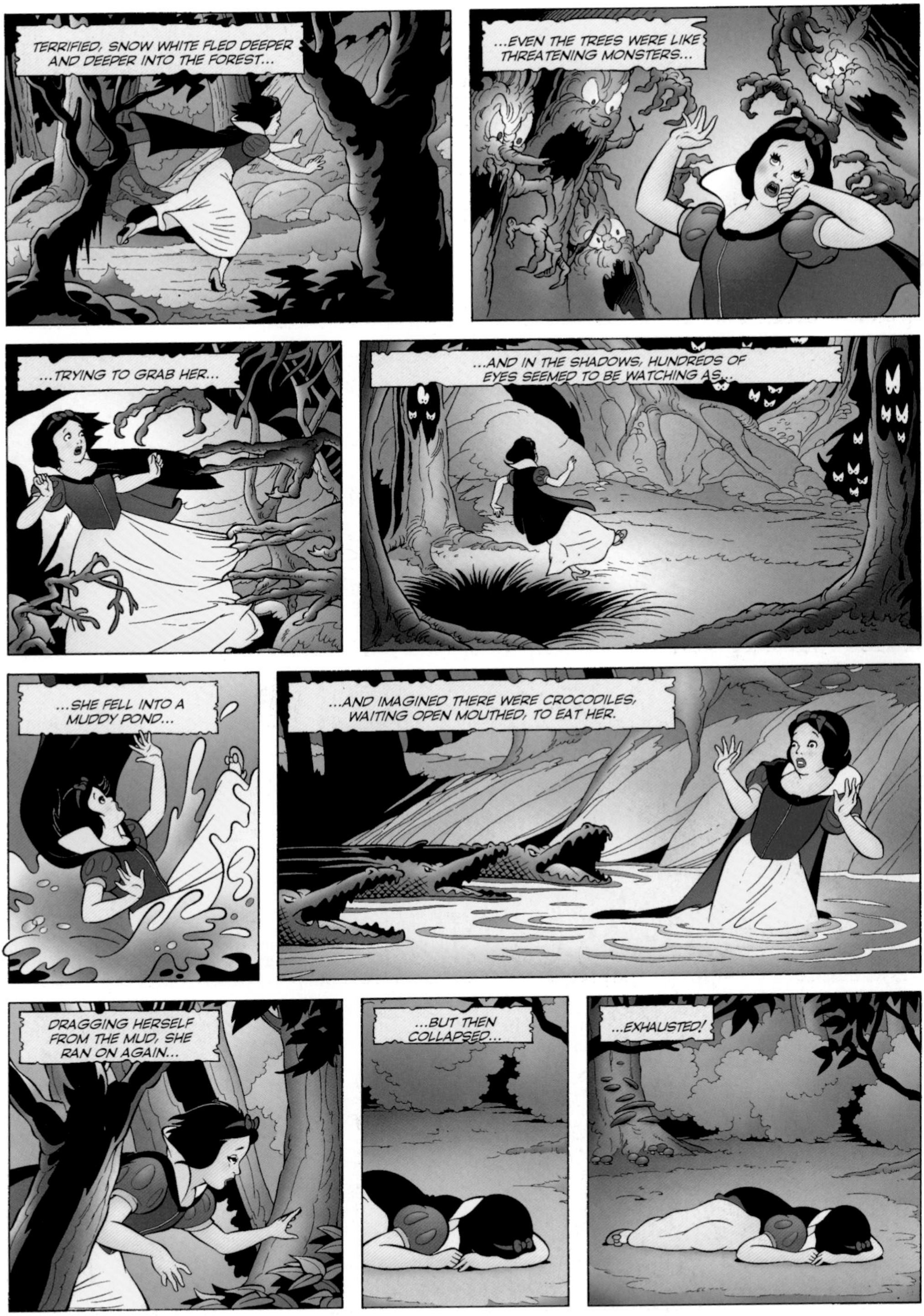
TERRIFIED, SNOW WHITE FLED DEEPER AND DEEPER INTO THE FOREST...
...EVEN THE TREES WERE LIKE THREATENING MONSTERS...
...TRYING TO GRAB HER...
...AND IN THE SHADOWS, HUNDREDS OF EYES SEEMED TO BE WATCHING AS...
...SHE FELL INTO A MUDDY POND...
...AND IMAGINED THERE WERE CROCODILES, WAITING OPEN MOUTHED, TO EAT HER.
DRAGGING HERSELF FROM THE MUD, SHE RAN ON AGAIN...
...BUT THEN COLLAPSED...
...EXHAUSTED!

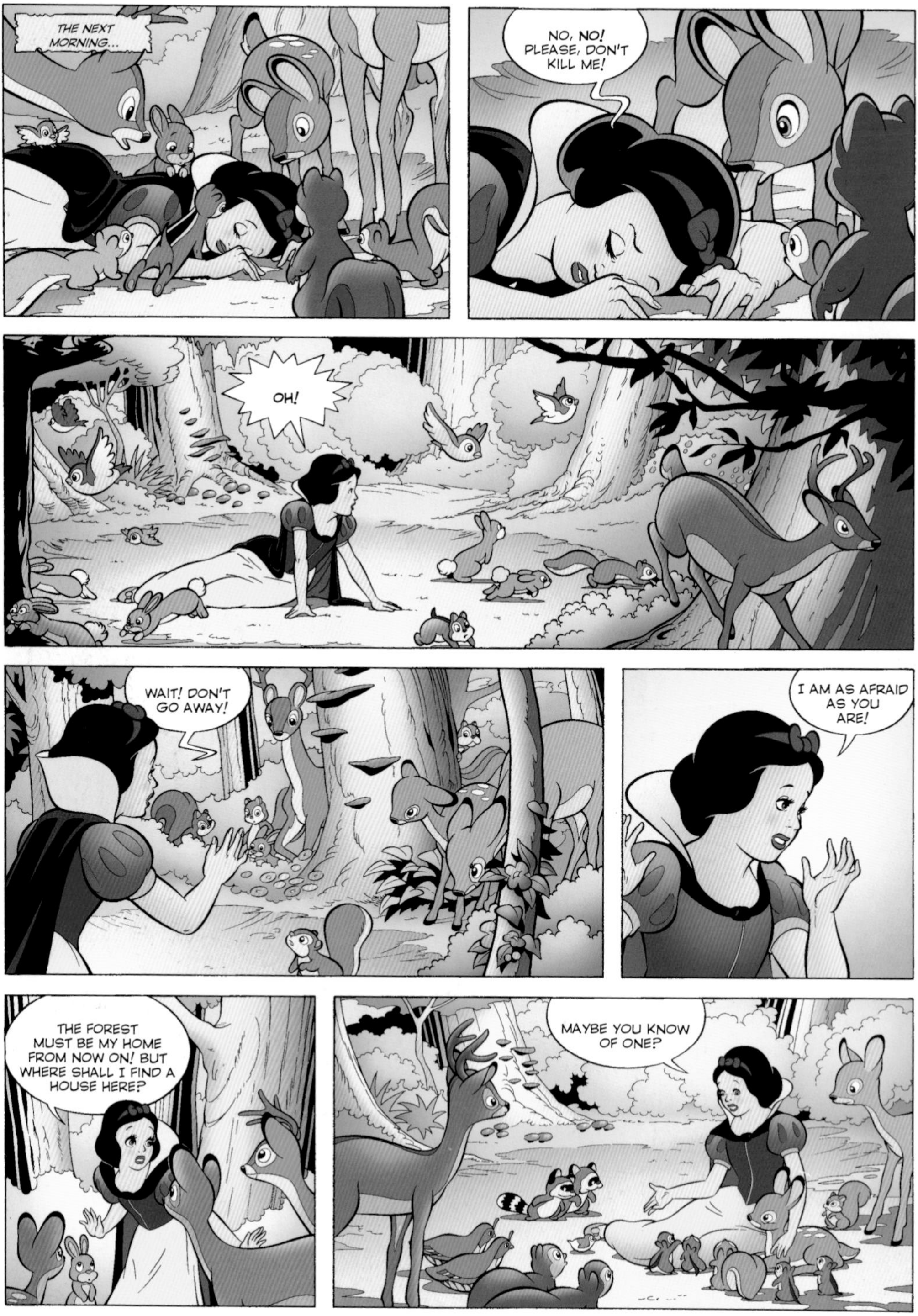
THE NEXT MORNING...
NO, NO! PLEASE, DON'T KILL ME!
OH!
WAIT! DON'T GO AWAY!
I AM AS AFRAID AS YOU ARE!
THE FOREST MUST BE MY HOME FROM NOW ON! BUT WHERE SHALL I FIND A HOUSE HERE?
MAYBE YOU KNOW OF ONE?

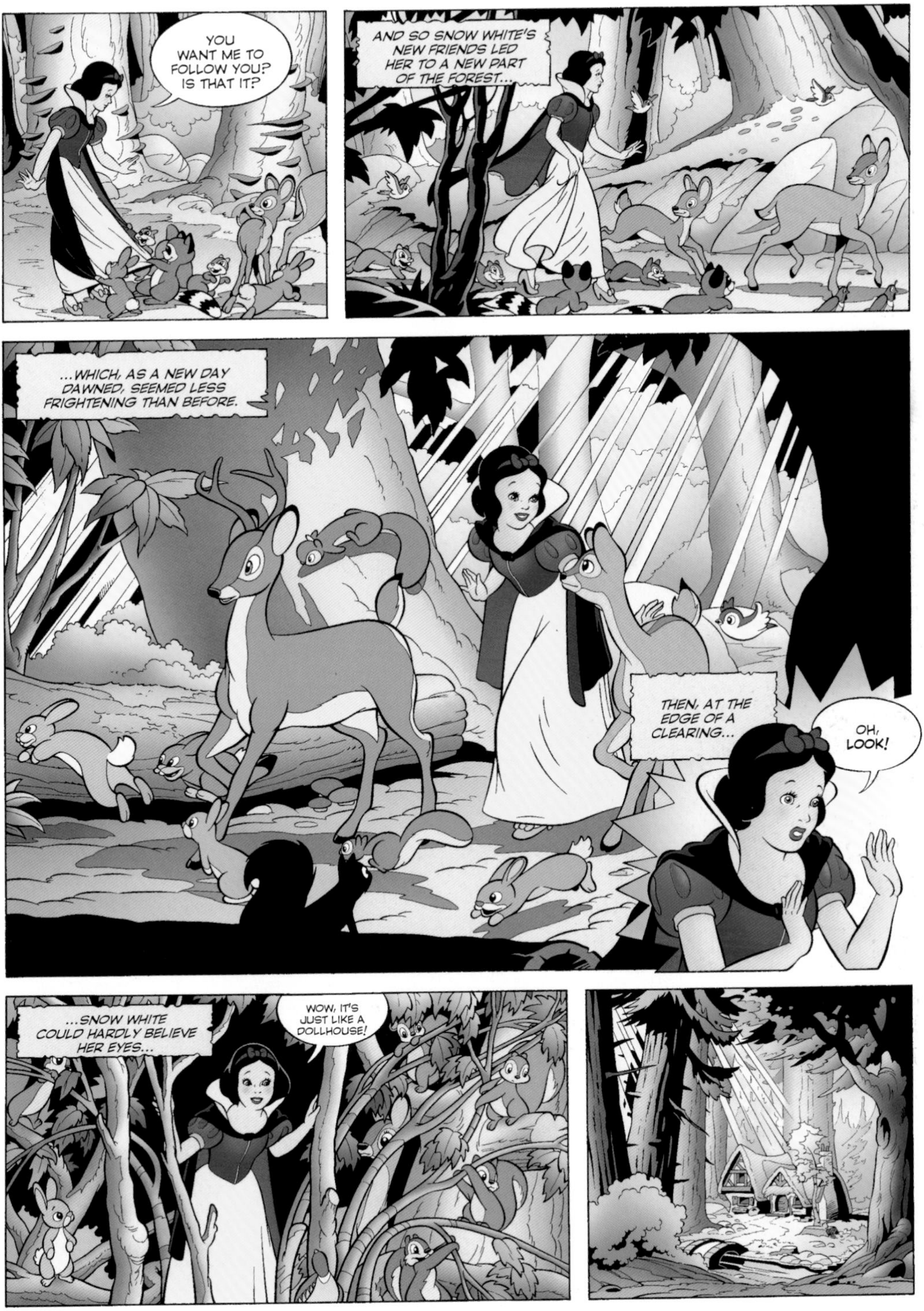
YOU WANT ME TO FOLLOW YOU? IS THAT IT?
AND SO SNOW WHITE'S NEW FRIENDS LED HER TO A NEW PART OF THE FOREST...
...WHICH, AS A NEW DAY DAWNED, SEEMED LESS FRIGHTENING THAN BEFORE.
THEN, AT THE EDGE OF A CLEARING...
OH, LOOK!
...SNOW WHITE COULD HARDLY BELIEVE HER EYES...
WOW, IT'S JUST LIKE A DOLLHOUSE!

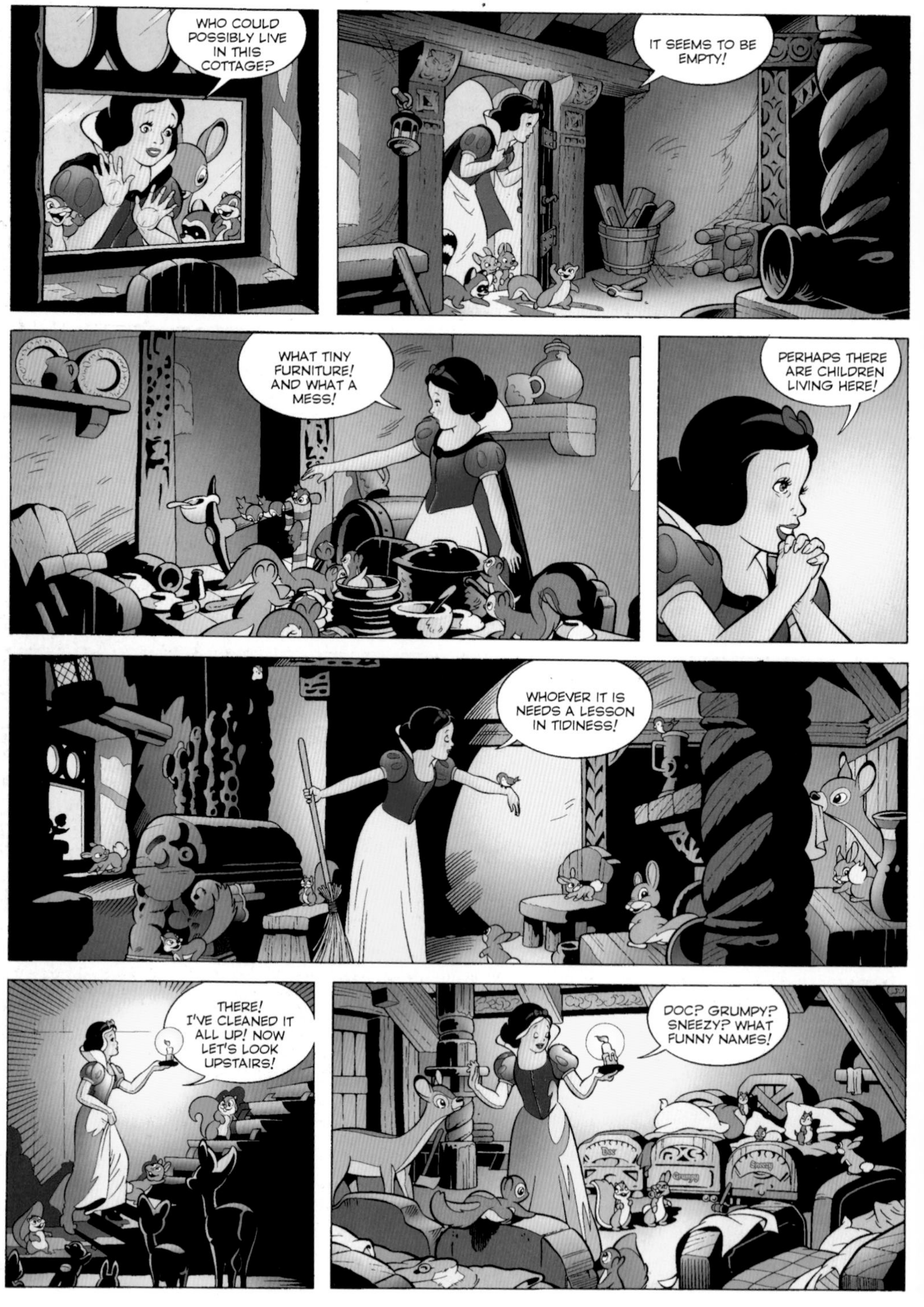
WHO COULD POSSIBLY LIVE IN THIS COTTAGE?
IT SEEMS TO BE EMPTY!
WHAT TINY FURNITURE! AND WHAT A MESS!
PERHAPS THERE ARE CHILDREN LIVING HERE!
WHOEVER IT IS NEEDS A LESSON IN TIDINESS!
THERE! I'VE CLEANED IT ALL UP! NOW LET'S LOOK UPSTAIRS!
DOC? GRUMPY? SNEEZY? WHAT FUNNY NAMES!
Doc
Grumpy
Sneezy

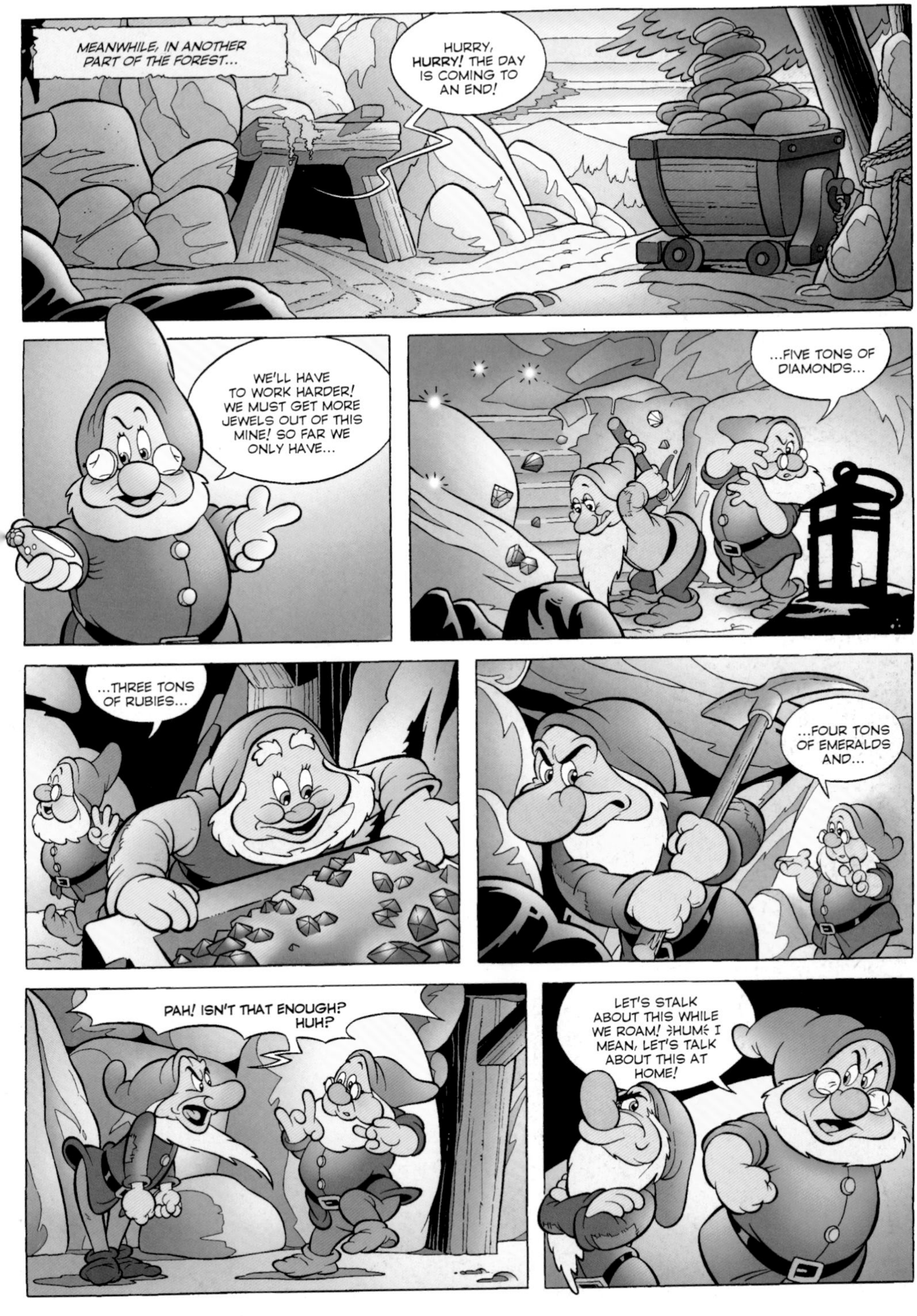
MEANWHILE, IN ANOTHER PART OF THE FOREST...
HURRY, HURRY! THE DAY IS COMING TO AN END!
WE'LL HAVE TO WORK HARDER! WE MUST GET MORE JEWELS OUT OF THIS MINE! SO FAR WE ONLY HAVE...
...FIVE TONS OF DIAMONDS...
...THREE TONS OF RUBIES...
...FOUR TONS OF EMERALDS AND...
PAH! ISN'T THAT ENOUGH?
HUH?
LET'S STALK ABOUT THIS WHILE WE ROAM! *HUM* I MEAN, LET'S TALK ABOUT THIS AT HOME!

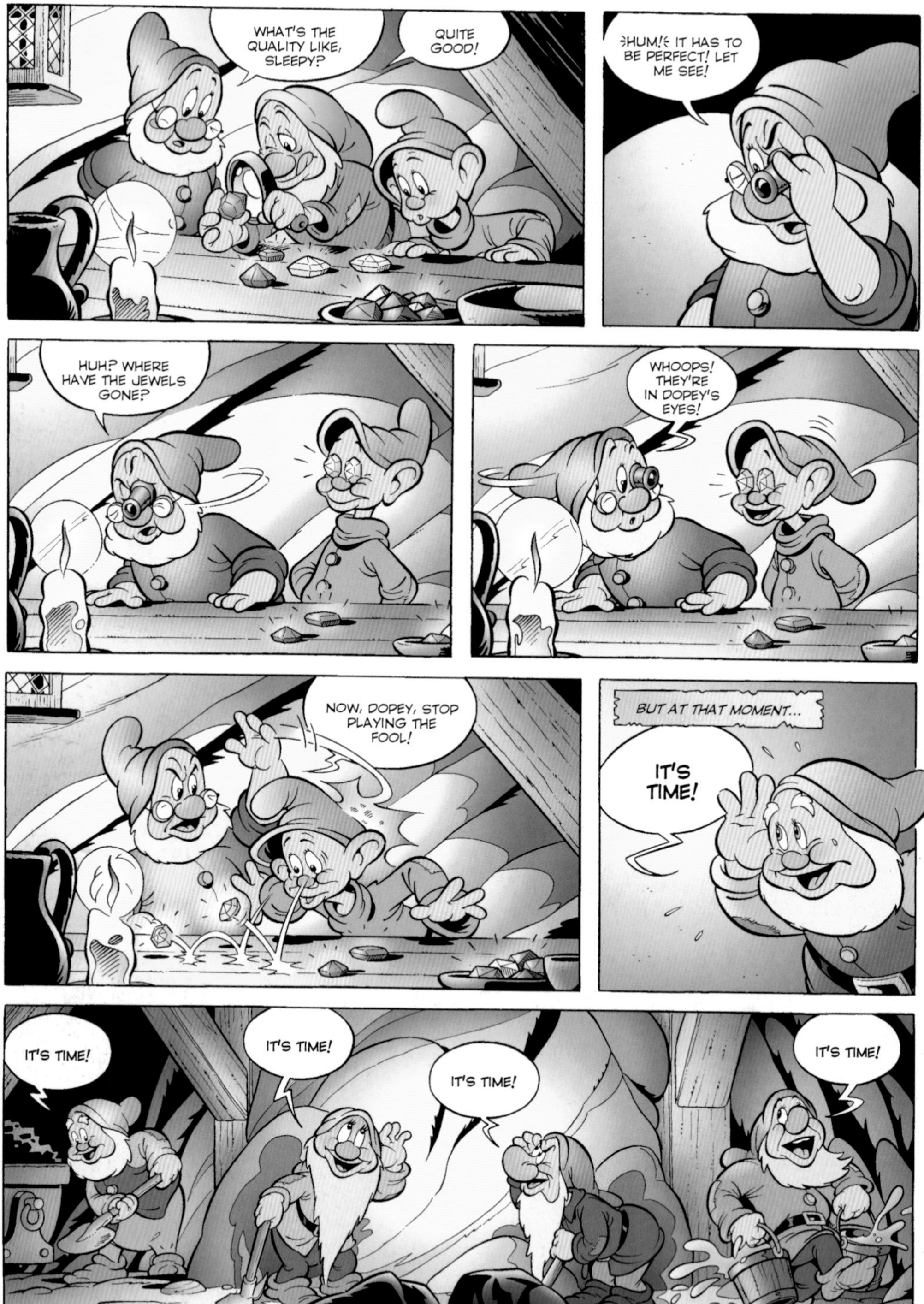
WHAT'S THE QUALITY LIKE, SLEEPY?
QUITE GOOD!
HUM! IT HAS TO BE PERFECT! LET ME SEE!
HUH? WHERE HAVE THE JEWELS GONE?
WHOOPS! THEY'RE IN DOPEY'S EYES!
NOW, DOPEY, STOP PLAYING THE FOOL!
BUT AT THAT MOMENT...
IT'S TIME!
IT'S TIME!
IT'S TIME!
IT'S TIME!
IT'S TIME!

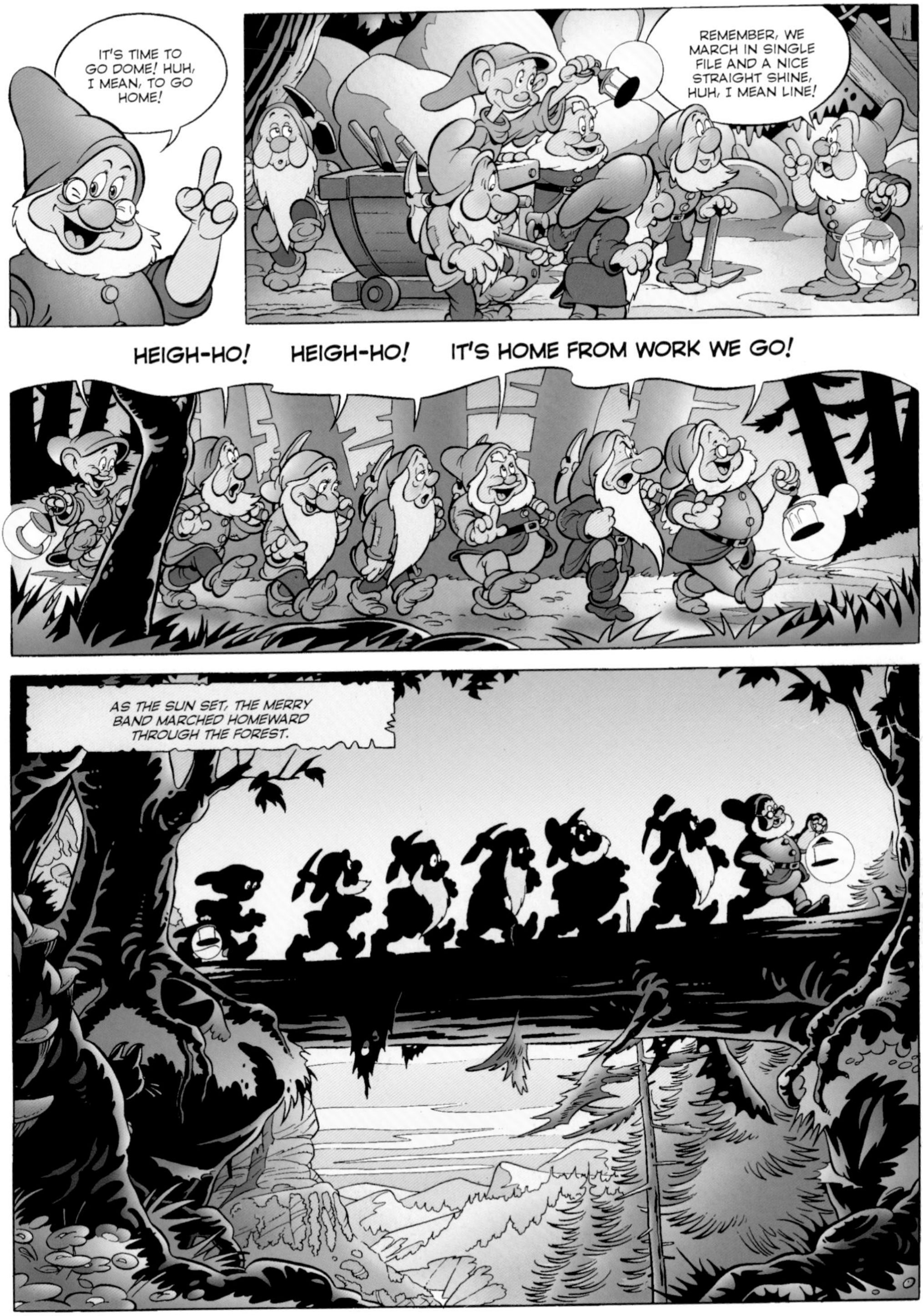
IT'S TIME TO GO DOME! HUH, I MEAN, TO GO HOME!
REMEMBER, WE MARCH IN SINGLE FILE AND A NICE STRAIGHT SHINE, HUH, I MEAN LINE!
HEIGH-HO! HEIGH-HO! IT'S HOME FROM WORK WE GO!
AS THE SUN SET, THE MERRY BAND MARCHED HOMEWARD THROUGH THE FOREST.

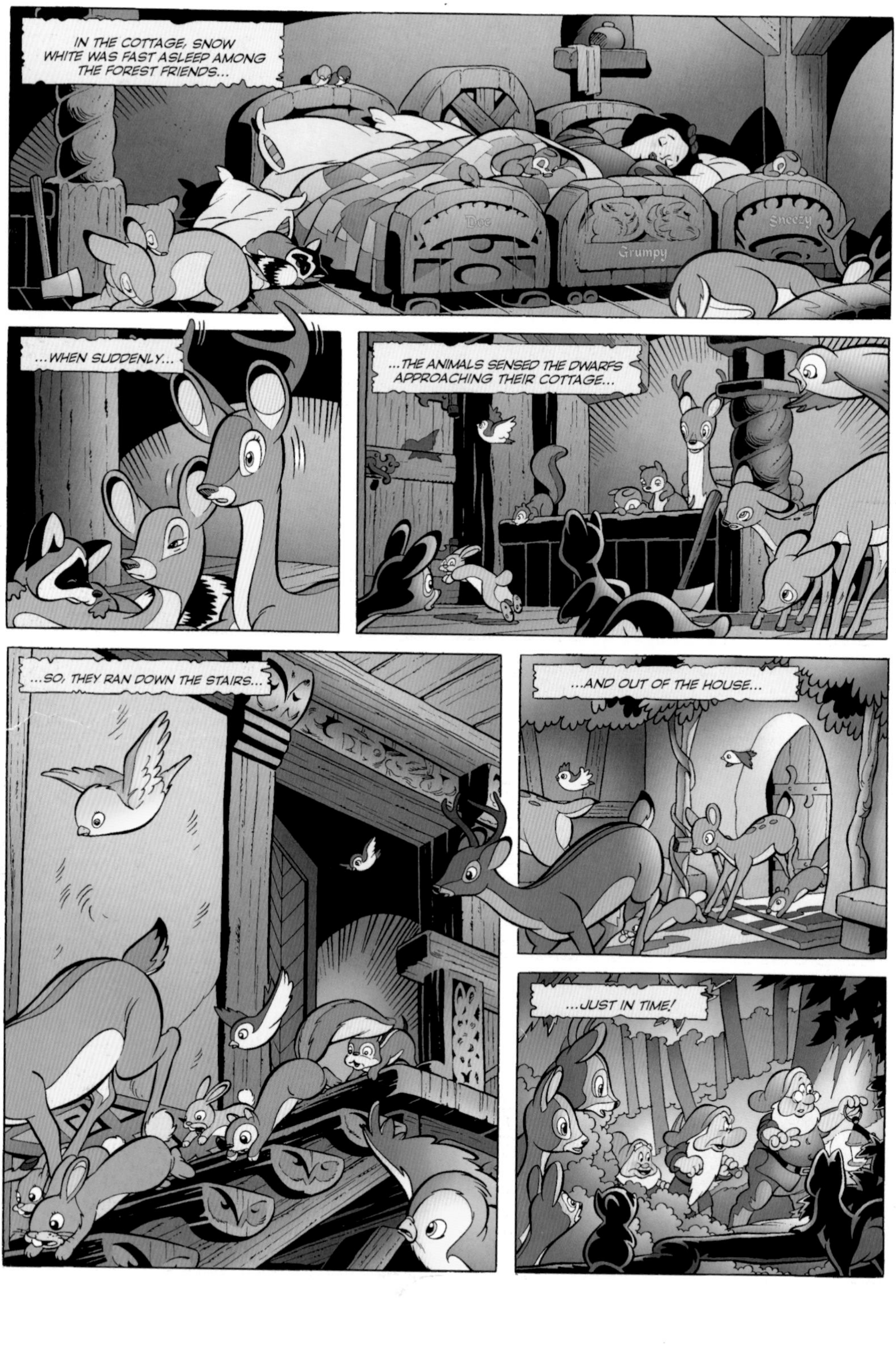
IN THE COTTAGE, SNOW WHITE WAS FAST ASLEEP AMONG THE FOREST FRIENDS...
Doc
Grumpy
Sneezy
...WHEN SUDDENLY...
...THE ANIMALS SENSED THE DWARFS APPROACHING THEIR COTTAGE...
...SO, THEY RAN DOWN THE STAIRS...
...AND OUT OF THE HOUSE...
...JUST IN TIME!

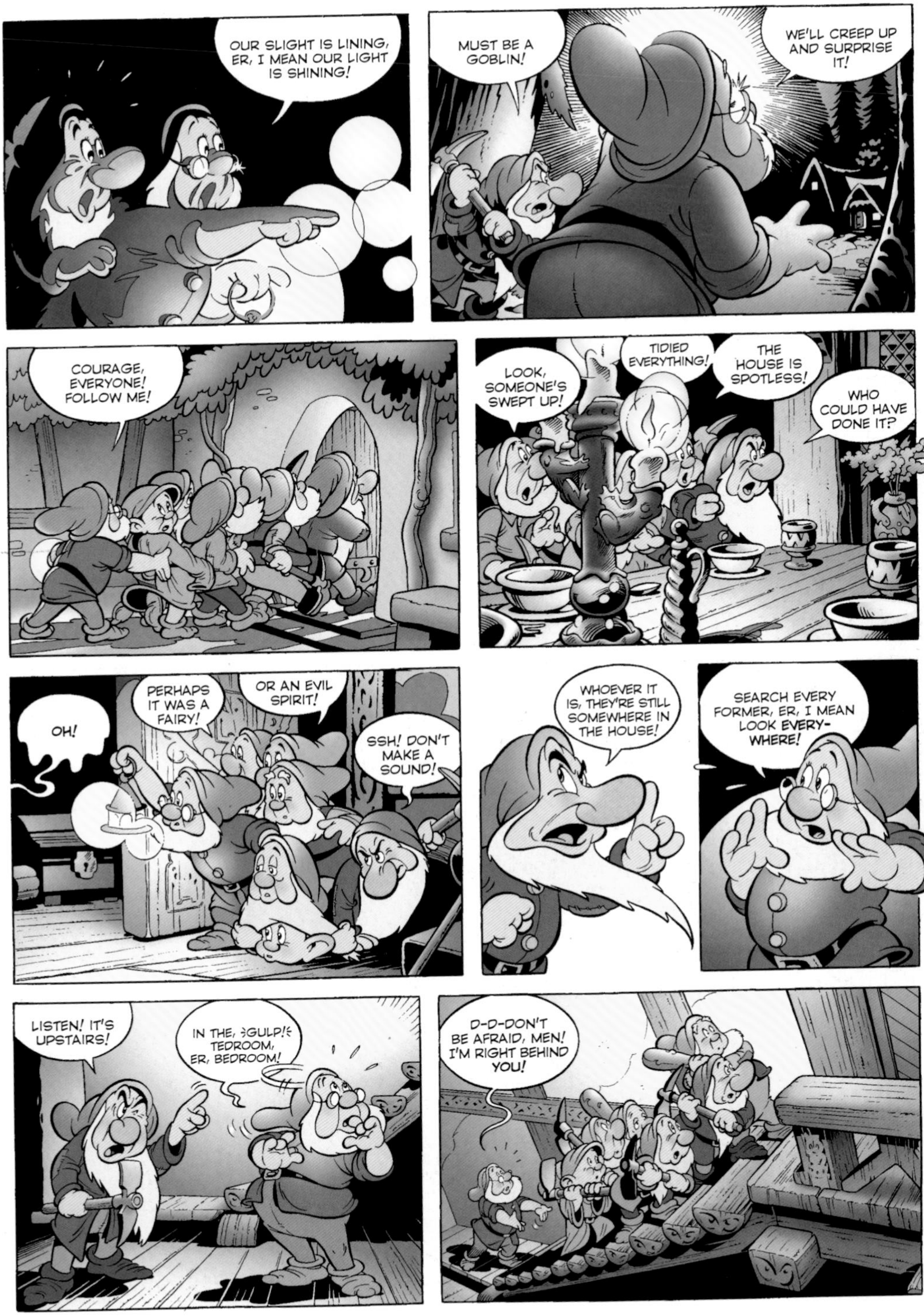
OUR SLIGHT IS LINING, ER, I MEAN OUR LIGHT IS SHINING!
MUST BE A GOBLIN!
WE'LL CREEP UP AND SURPRISE IT!
COURAGE, EVERYONE! FOLLOW ME!
LOOK, SOMEONE'S SWEPT UP!
TIDIED EVERYTHING!
THE HOUSE IS SPOTLESS!
WHO COULD HAVE DONE IT?
OH!
PERHAPS IT WAS A FAIRY!
OR AN EVIL SPIRIT!
SSH! DON'T MAKE A SOUND!
WHOEVER IT IS, THEY'RE STILL SOMEWHERE IN THE HOUSE!
SEARCH EVERY FORMER, ER, I MEAN LOOK EVERY-WHERE!
LISTEN! IT'S UPSTAIRS!
IN THE, GULP! TEDROOM, ER, BEDROOM!
D-D-DON'T BE AFRAID, MEN! I'M RIGHT BEHIND YOU!

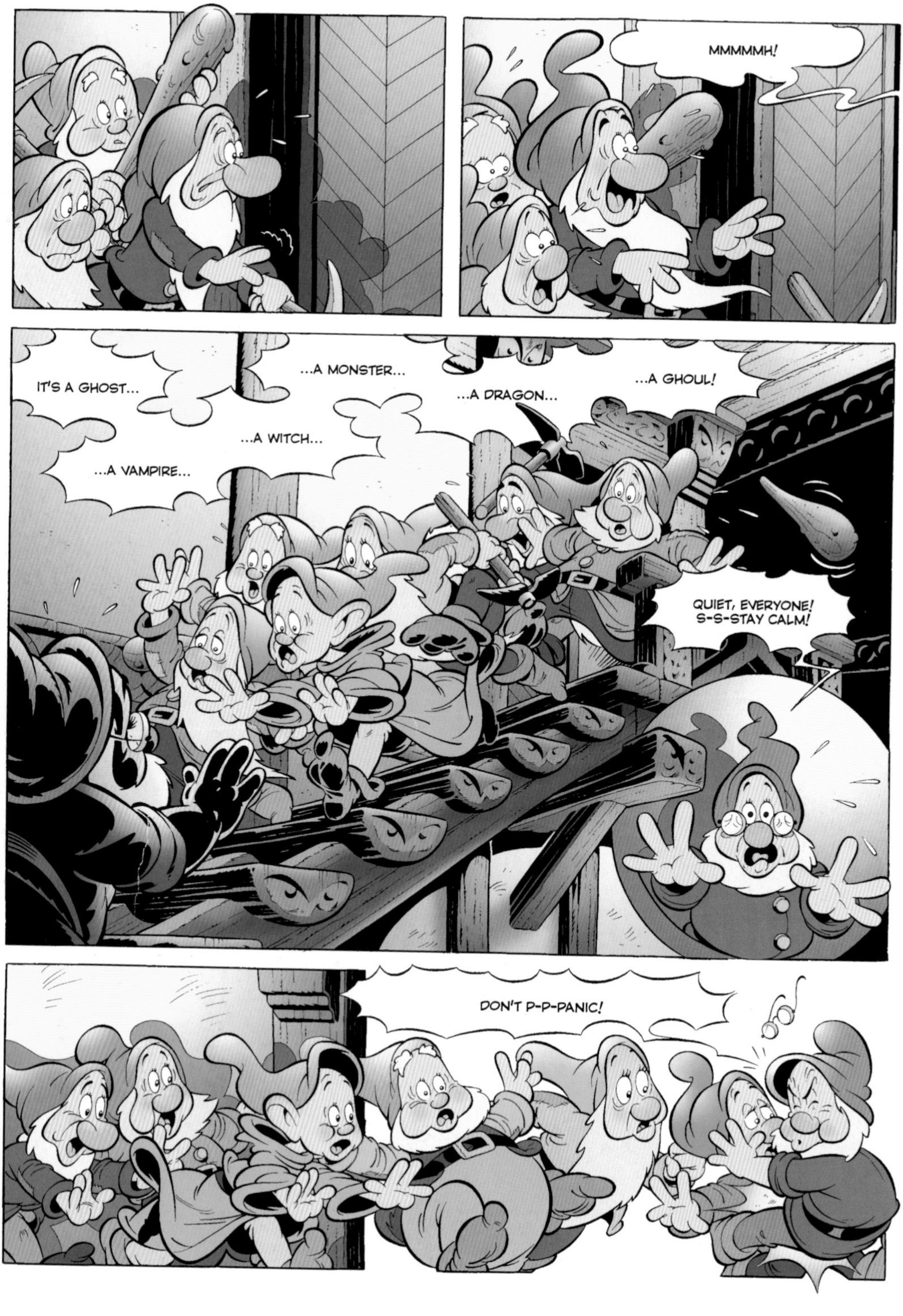
MMMMMH!
IT'S A GHOST...
...A MONSTER...
...A VAMPIRE...
...A WITCH...
...A DRAGON...
...A GHOUL!
QUIET, EVERYONE! S-S-STAY CALM!
DON'T P-P-PANIC!

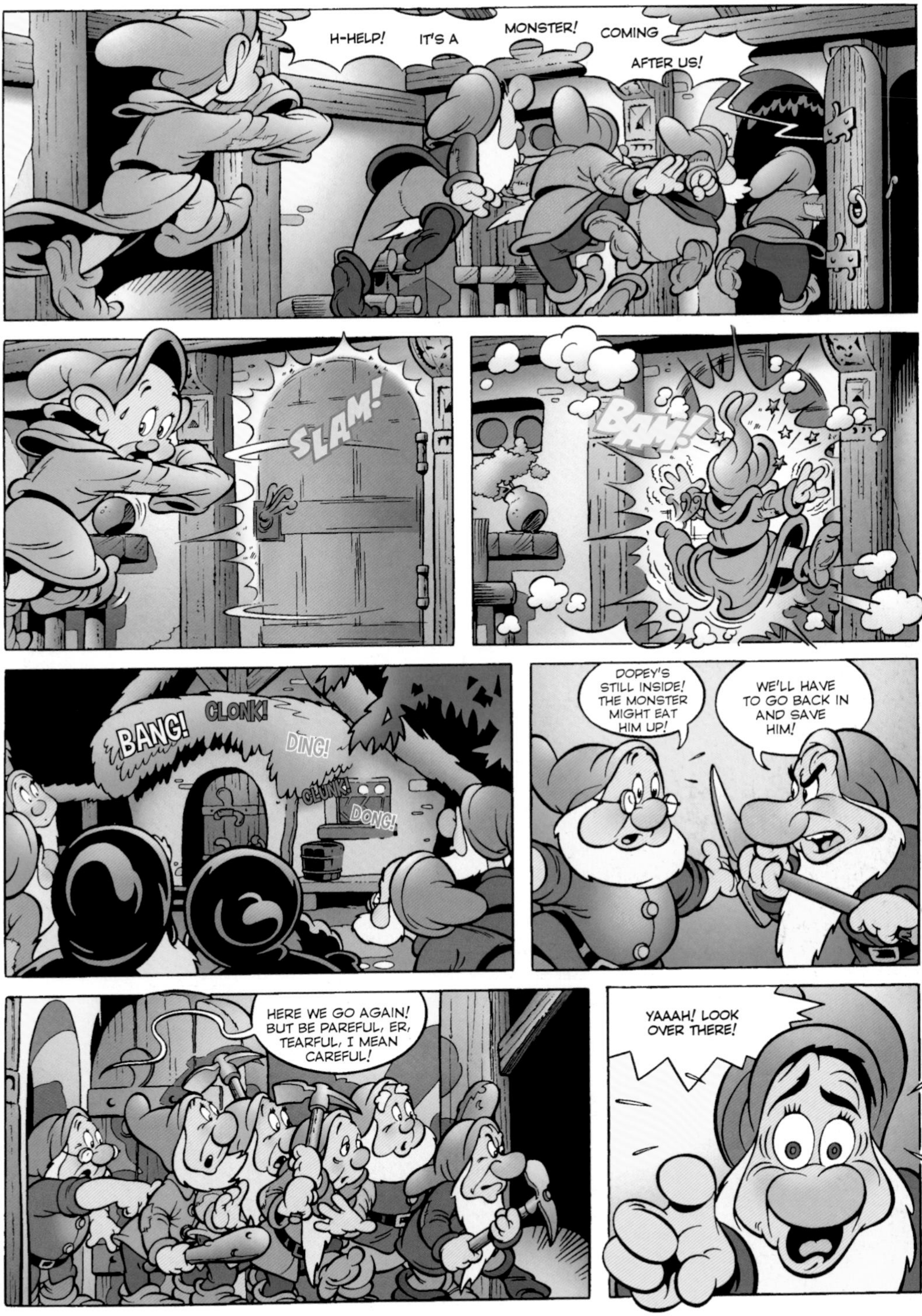
H-HELP!
IT'S A
MONSTER!
COMING
AFTER US!
SLAM!
BAM!
BANG!
CLONK!
DING!
CLUNK!
DONG!
DOPEY'S STILL INSIDE! THE MONSTER MIGHT EAT HIM UP!
WE'LL HAVE TO GO BACK IN AND SAVE HIM!
HERE WE GO AGAIN! BUT BE PAREFUL, ER, TEARFUL, I MEAN CAREFUL!
YAAAH! LOOK OVER THERE!

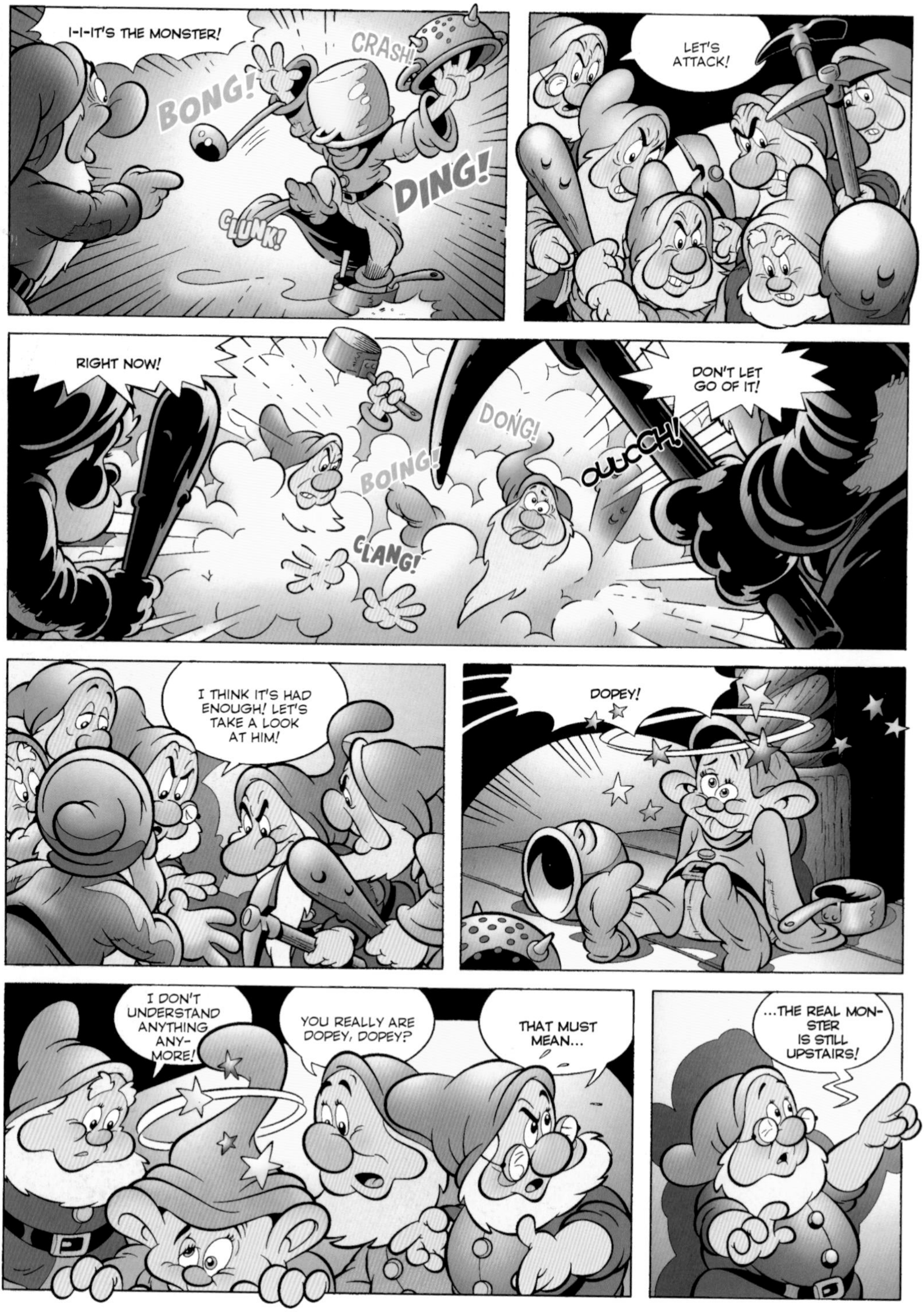
I-I-IT'S THE MONSTER!
CRASH!
BONG!
DING!
CLUNK!
LET'S ATTACK!
RIGHT NOW!
DON'T LET GO OF IT!
DONG!
BOING!
OUUCCH!
CLANG!
I THINK IT'S HAD ENOUGH! LET'S TAKE A LOOK AT HIM!
DOPEY!
I DON'T UNDERSTAND ANYTHING ANY-MORE!
YOU REALLY ARE DOPEY, DOPEY?
THAT MUST MEAN...
...THE REAL MON-STER IS STILL UPSTAIRS!

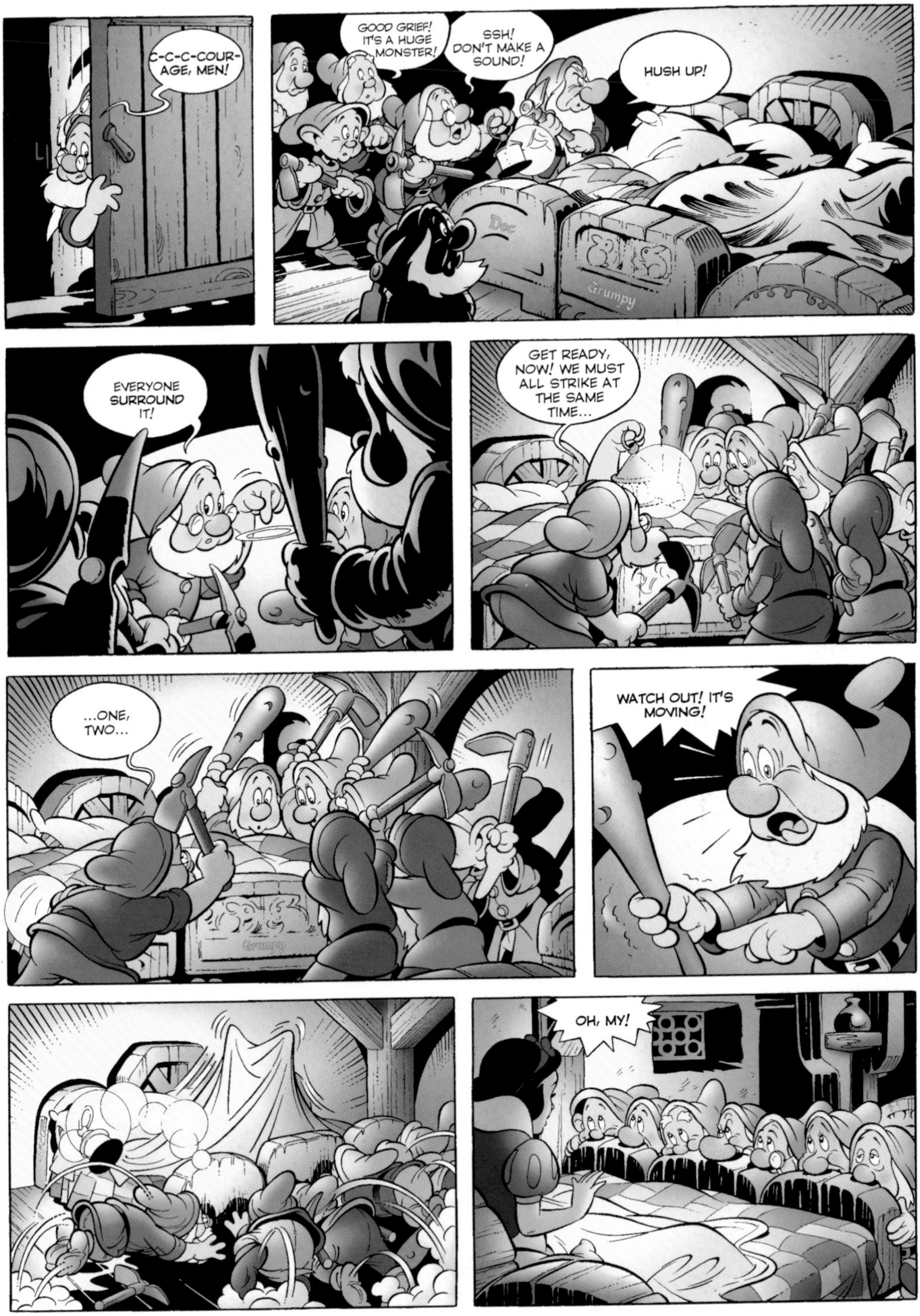
C-C-C-COURAGE, MEN!
GOOD GRIEF! IT'S A HUGE MONSTER!
SSH! DON'T MAKE A SOUND!
HUSH UP!
Doc
Grumpy
EVERYONE SURROUND IT!
GET READY, NOW! WE MUST ALL STRIKE AT THE SAME TIME...
...ONE, TWO...
Grumpy
WATCH OUT! IT'S MOVING!
OH, MY!

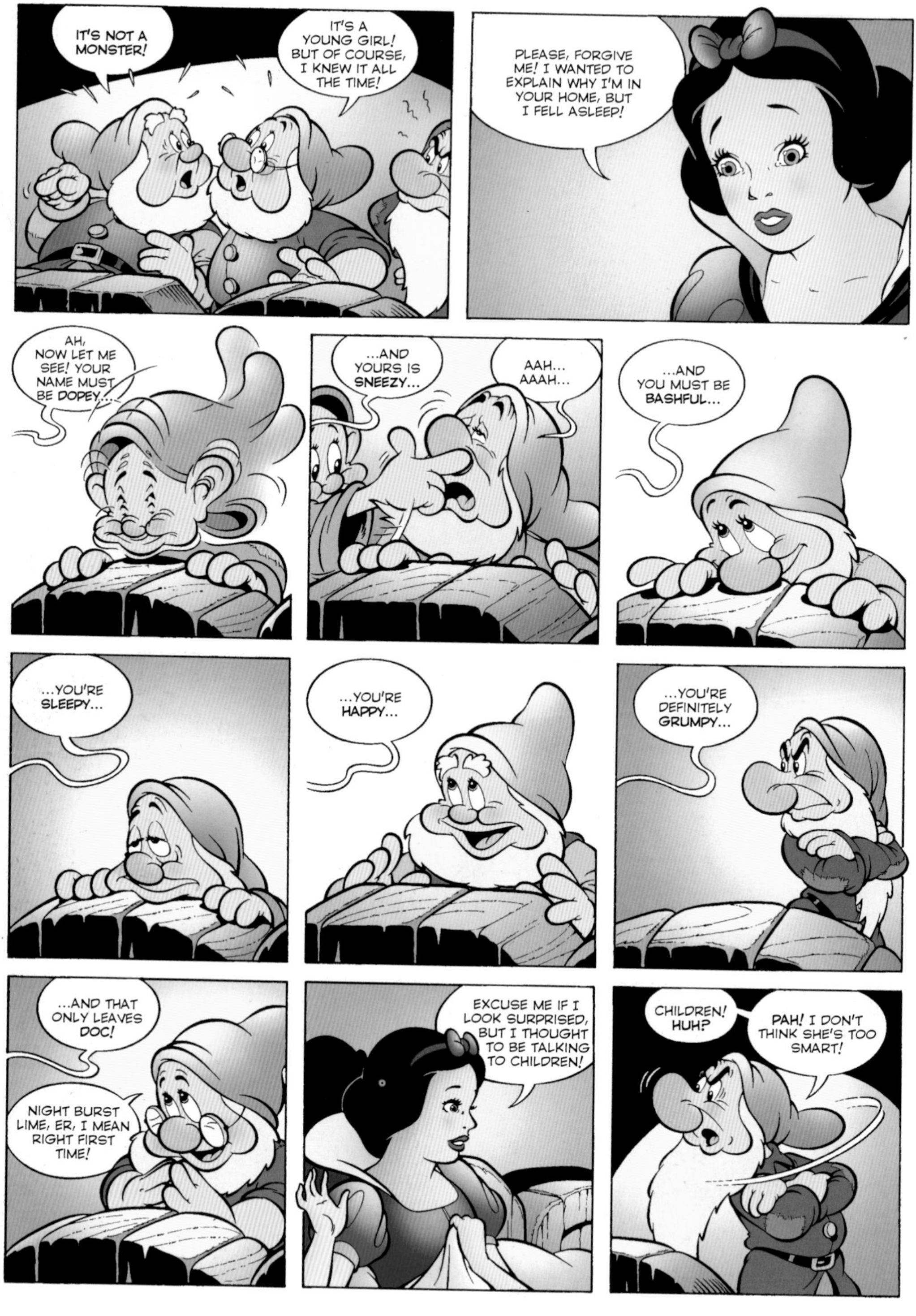
IT'S NOT A MONSTER!
IT'S A YOUNG GIRL! BUT OF COURSE, I KNEW IT ALL THE TIME!
PLEASE, FORGIVE ME! I WANTED TO EXPLAIN WHY I'M IN YOUR HOME, BUT I FELL ASLEEP!
AH, NOW LET ME SEE! YOUR NAME MUST BE DOPEY...
...AND YOURS IS SNEEZY...
AAH... AAAH...
...AND YOU MUST BE BASHFUL...
...YOU'RE SLEEPY...
...YOU'RE HAPPY...
...YOU'RE DEFINITELY GRUMPY...
...AND THAT ONLY LEAVES DOC!
NIGHT BURST LIME, ER, I MEAN RIGHT FIRST TIME!
EXCUSE ME IF I LOOK SURPRISED, BUT I THOUGHT TO BE TALKING TO CHILDREN!
CHILDREN! HUH?
PAH! I DON'T THINK SHE'S TOO SMART!

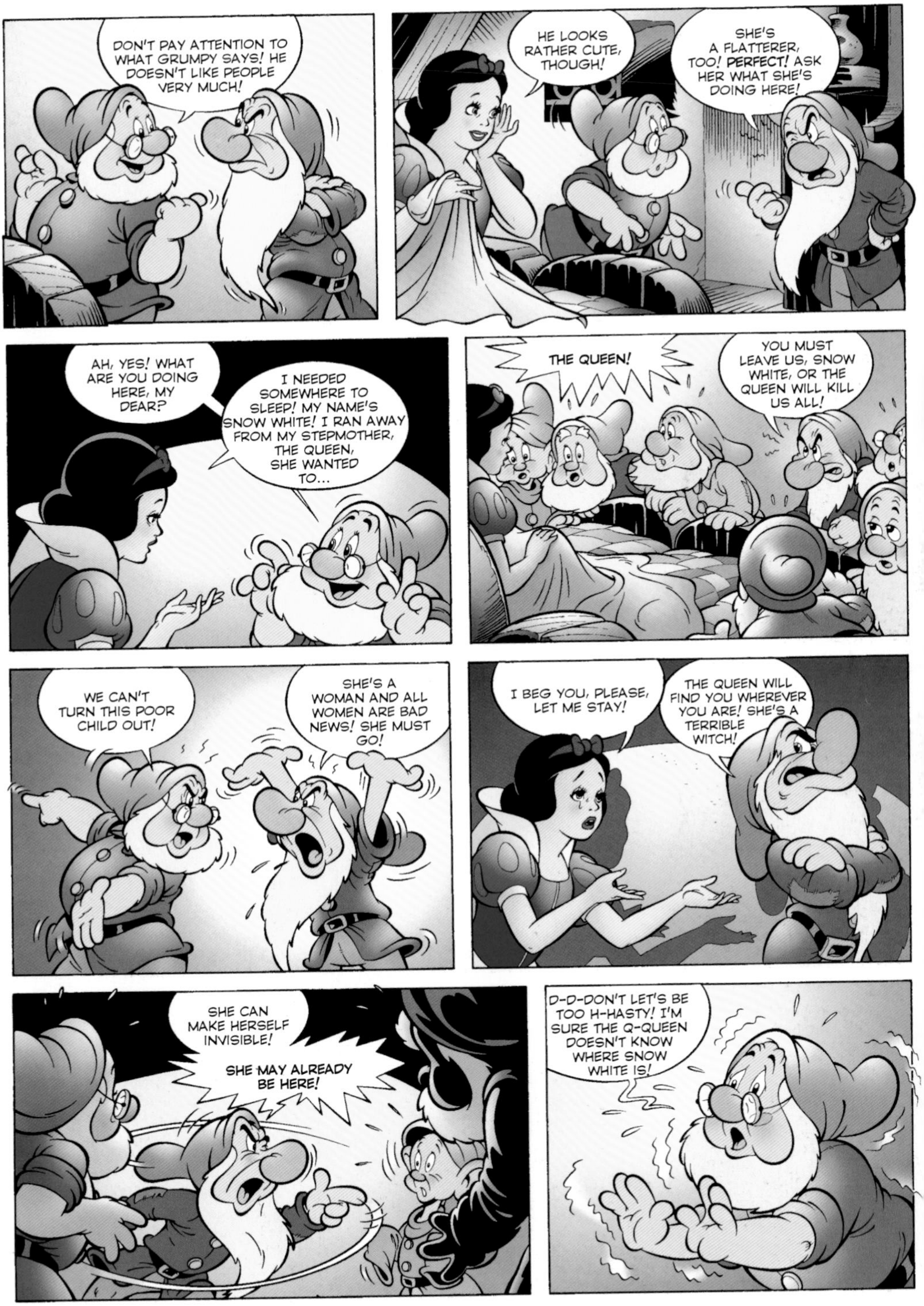
DON'T PAY ATTENTION TO WHAT GRUMPY SAYS! HE DOESN'T LIKE PEOPLE VERY MUCH!
HE LOOKS RATHER CUTE, THOUGH!
SHE'S A FLATTERER, TOO! PERFECT! ASK HER WHAT SHE'S DOING HERE!
AH, YES! WHAT ARE YOU DOING HERE, MY DEAR?
I NEEDED SOMEWHERE TO SLEEP! MY NAME'S SNOW WHITE! I RAN AWAY FROM MY STEPMOTHER, THE QUEEN, SHE WANTED TO...
THE QUEEN!
YOU MUST LEAVE US, SNOW WHITE, OR THE QUEEN WILL KILL US ALL!
WE CAN'T TURN THIS POOR CHILD OUT!
SHE'S A WOMAN AND ALL WOMEN ARE BAD NEWS! SHE MUST GO!
I BEG YOU, PLEASE, LET ME STAY!
THE QUEEN WILL FIND YOU WHEREVER YOU ARE! SHE'S A TERRIBLE WITCH!
SHE CAN MAKE HERSELF INVISIBLE!
SHE MAY ALREADY BE HERE!
D-D-DON'T LET'S BE TOO H-HASTY! I'M SURE THE Q-QUEEN DOESN'T KNOW WHERE SNOW WHITE IS!

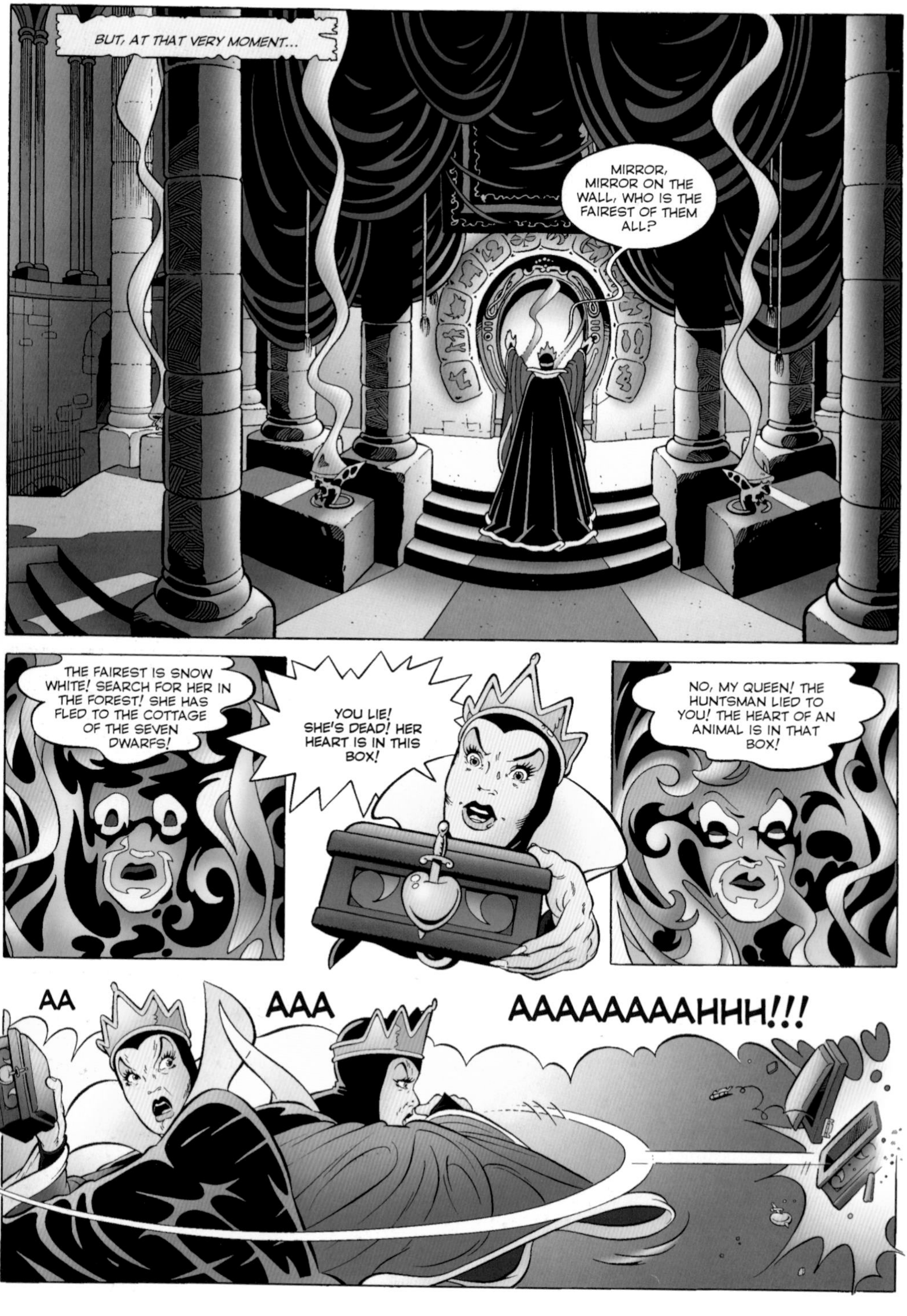
BUT, AT THAT VERY MOMENT...
MIRROR, MIRROR ON THE WALL, WHO IS THE FAIREST OF THEM ALL?
THE FAIREST IS SNOW WHITE! SEARCH FOR HER IN THE FOREST! SHE HAS FLED TO THE COTTAGE OF THE SEVEN DWARFS!
YOU LIE! SHE'S DEAD! HER HEART IS IN THIS BOX!
NO, MY QUEEN! THE HUNTSMAN LIED TO YOU! THE HEART OF AN ANIMAL IS IN THAT BOX!
AA
AAA
AAAAAAAAHHH!!!

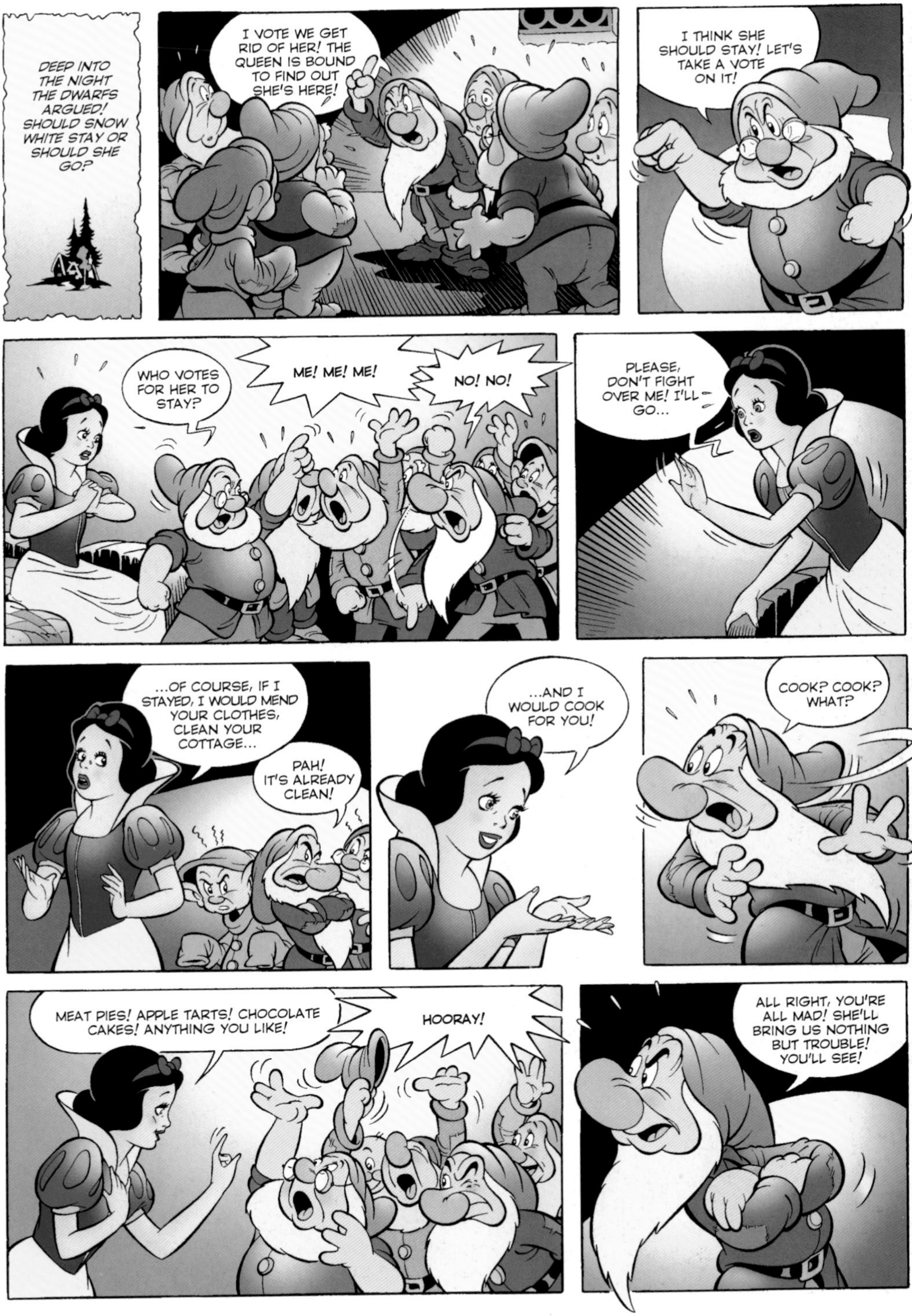
DEEP INTO THE NIGHT THE DWARFS ARGUED! SHOULD SNOW WHITE STAY OR SHOULD SHE GO?
I VOTE WE GET RID OF HER! THE QUEEN IS BOUND TO FIND OUT SHE'S HERE!
I THINK SHE SHOULD STAY! LET'S TAKE A VOTE ON IT!
WHO VOTES FOR HER TO STAY?
ME! ME! ME!
NO! NO!
PLEASE, DON'T FIGHT OVER ME! I'LL GO...
...OF COURSE, IF I STAYED, I WOULD MEND YOUR CLOTHES, CLEAN YOUR COTTAGE...
PAH! IT'S ALREADY CLEAN!
...AND I WOULD COOK FOR YOU!
COOK? COOK? WHAT?
MEAT PIES! APPLE TARTS! CHOCOLATE CAKES! ANYTHING YOU LIKE!
HOORAY!
ALL RIGHT, YOU'RE ALL MAD! SHE'LL BRING US NOTHING BUT TROUBLE! YOU'LL SEE!

IN HER CASTLE, THE EVIL QUEEN WAS PREPARING A MAGIC POTION...

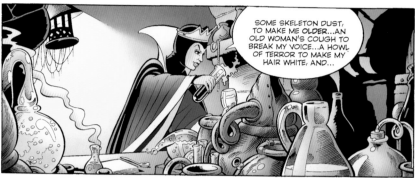

SOME SKELETON DUST, TO MAKE ME OLDER...AN OLD WOMAN'S COUGH TO BREAK MY VOICE...A HOWL OF TERROR TO MAKE MY HAIR WHITE, AND...

...ONE DRINK OF THIS MAGIC BREW, THEN I WILL BE SO TRANSFORMED, SNOW WHITE...

...WILL NEVER RECOGNIZE ME!

AH!

HOW DO I LOOK, MY PRECIOUS ONE?

BECOMING OLD AND WRINKLED?

?

CRAW! CRAW!

}UURGH!{

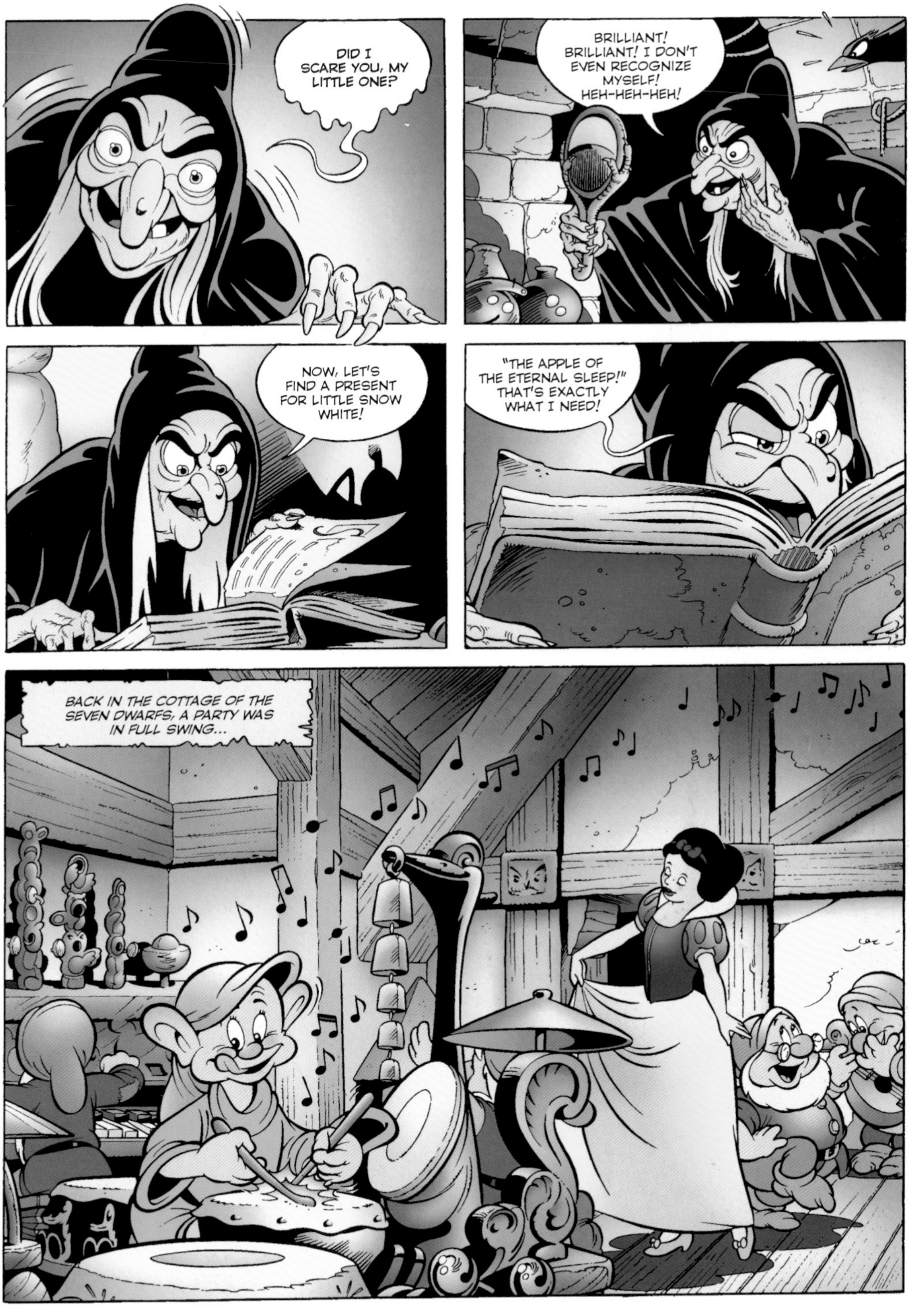
DID I SCARE YOU, MY LITTLE ONE?
BRILLIANT! BRILLIANT! I DON'T EVEN RECOGNIZE MYSELF! HEH-HEH-HEH!
NOW, LET'S FIND A PRESENT FOR LITTLE SNOW WHITE!
"THE APPLE OF THE ETERNAL SLEEP!" THAT'S EXACTLY WHAT I NEED!
BACK IN THE COTTAGE OF THE SEVEN DWARFS, A PARTY WAS IN FULL SWING...

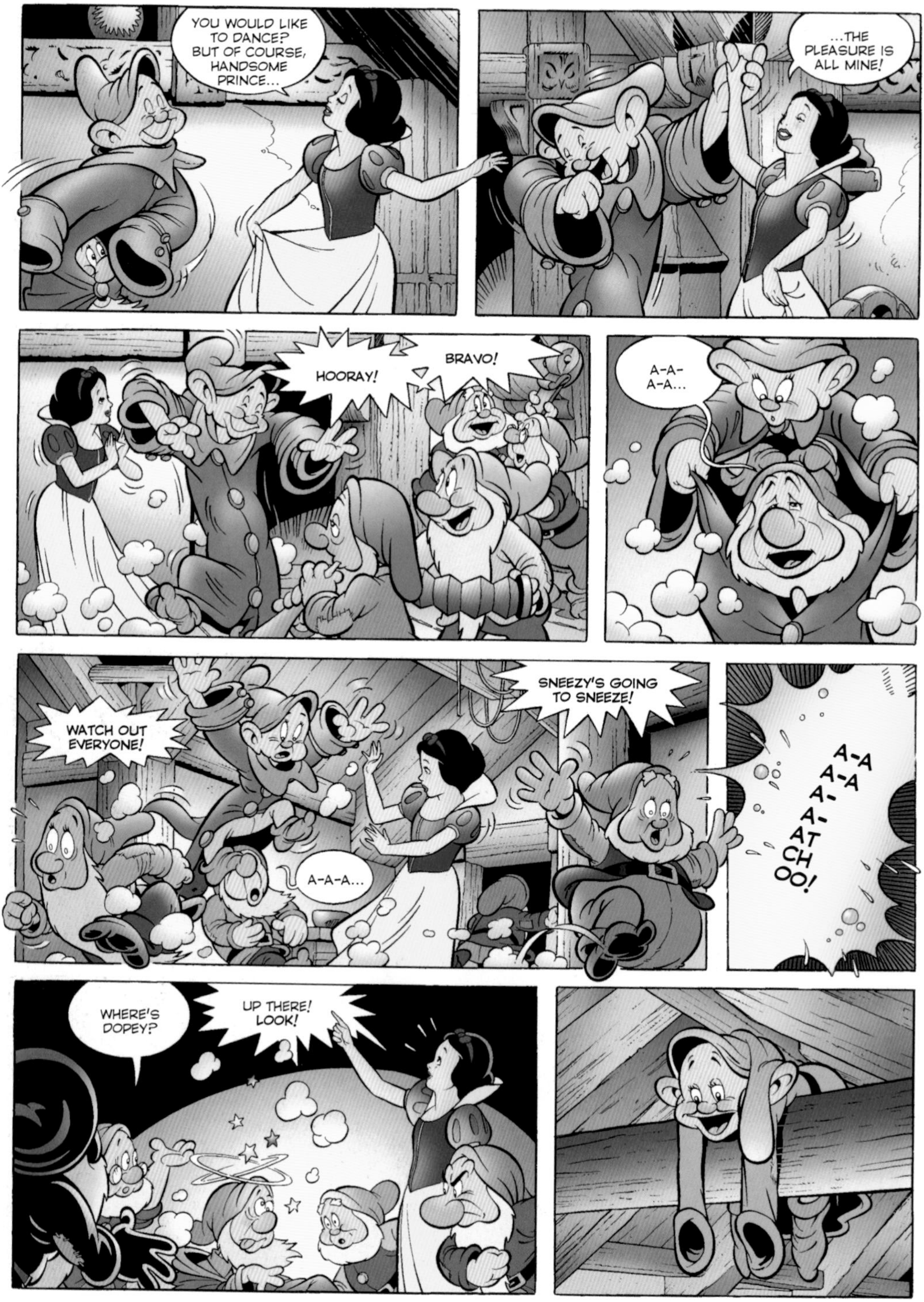

YOU WOULD LIKE TO DANCE? BUT OF COURSE, HANDSOME PRINCE...
...THE PLEASURE IS ALL MINE!
HOORAY!
BRAVO!
A-A-A-A...
WATCH OUT EVERYONE!
A-A-A...
SNEEZY'S GOING TO SNEEZE!
A-A A-A A- A- ATCHOO!
WHERE'S DOPEY?
UP THERE! LOOK!

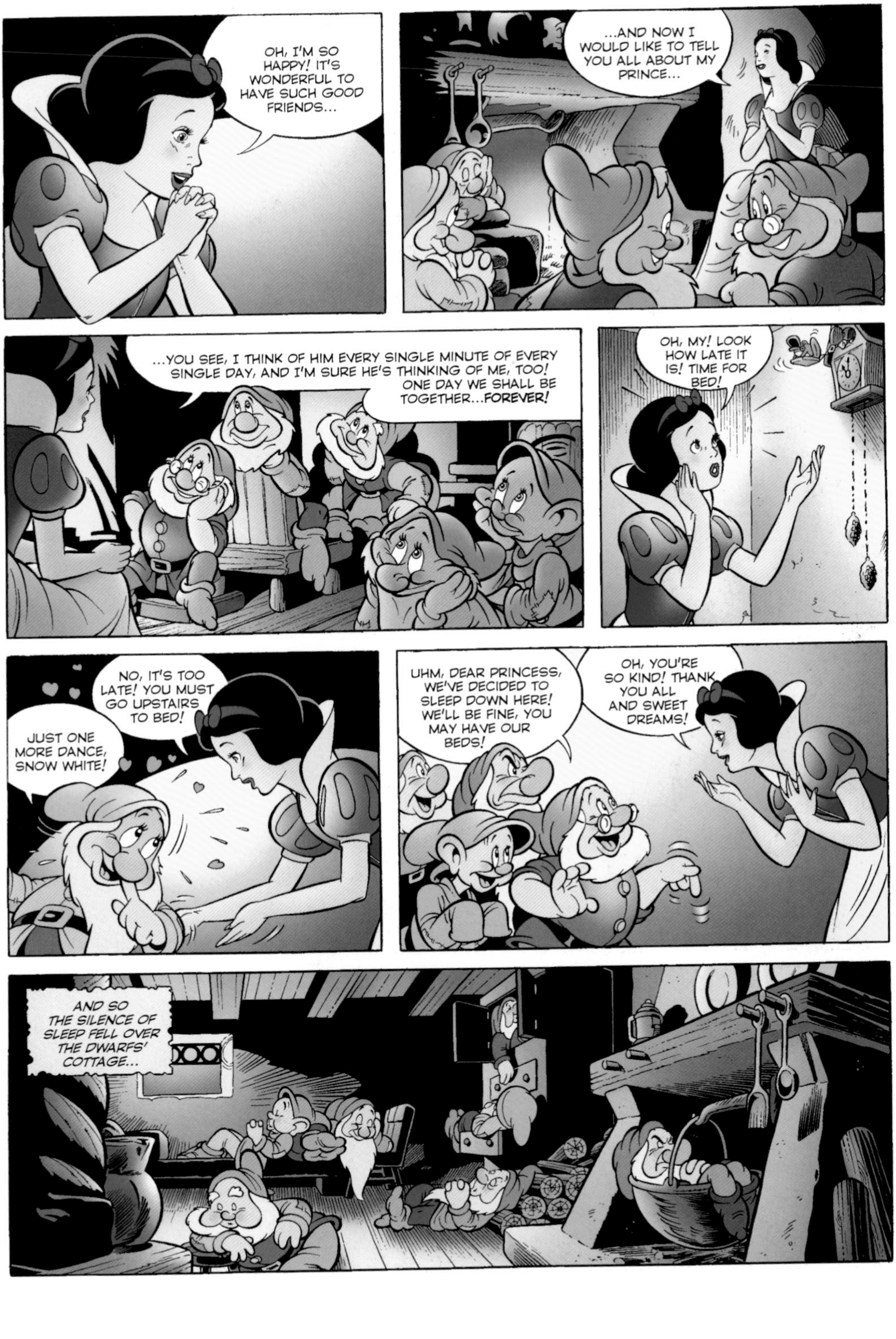
OH, I'M SO HAPPY! IT'S WONDERFUL TO HAVE SUCH GOOD FRIENDS...
...AND NOW I WOULD LIKE TO TELL YOU ALL ABOUT MY PRINCE...
...YOU SEE, I THINK OF HIM EVERY SINGLE MINUTE OF EVERY SINGLE DAY, AND I'M SURE HE'S THINKING OF ME, TOO! ONE DAY WE SHALL BE TOGETHER...FOREVER!
OH, MY! LOOK HOW LATE IT IS! TIME FOR BED!
JUST ONE MORE DANCE, SNOW WHITE!
NO, IT'S TOO LATE! YOU MUST GO UPSTAIRS TO BED!
UHM, DEAR PRINCESS, WE'VE DECIDED TO SLEEP DOWN HERE! WE'LL BE FINE, YOU MAY HAVE OUR BEDS!
OH, YOU'RE SO KIND! THANK YOU ALL AND SWEET DREAMS!
AND SO THE SILENCE OF SLEEP FELL OVER THE DWARFS' COTTAGE...

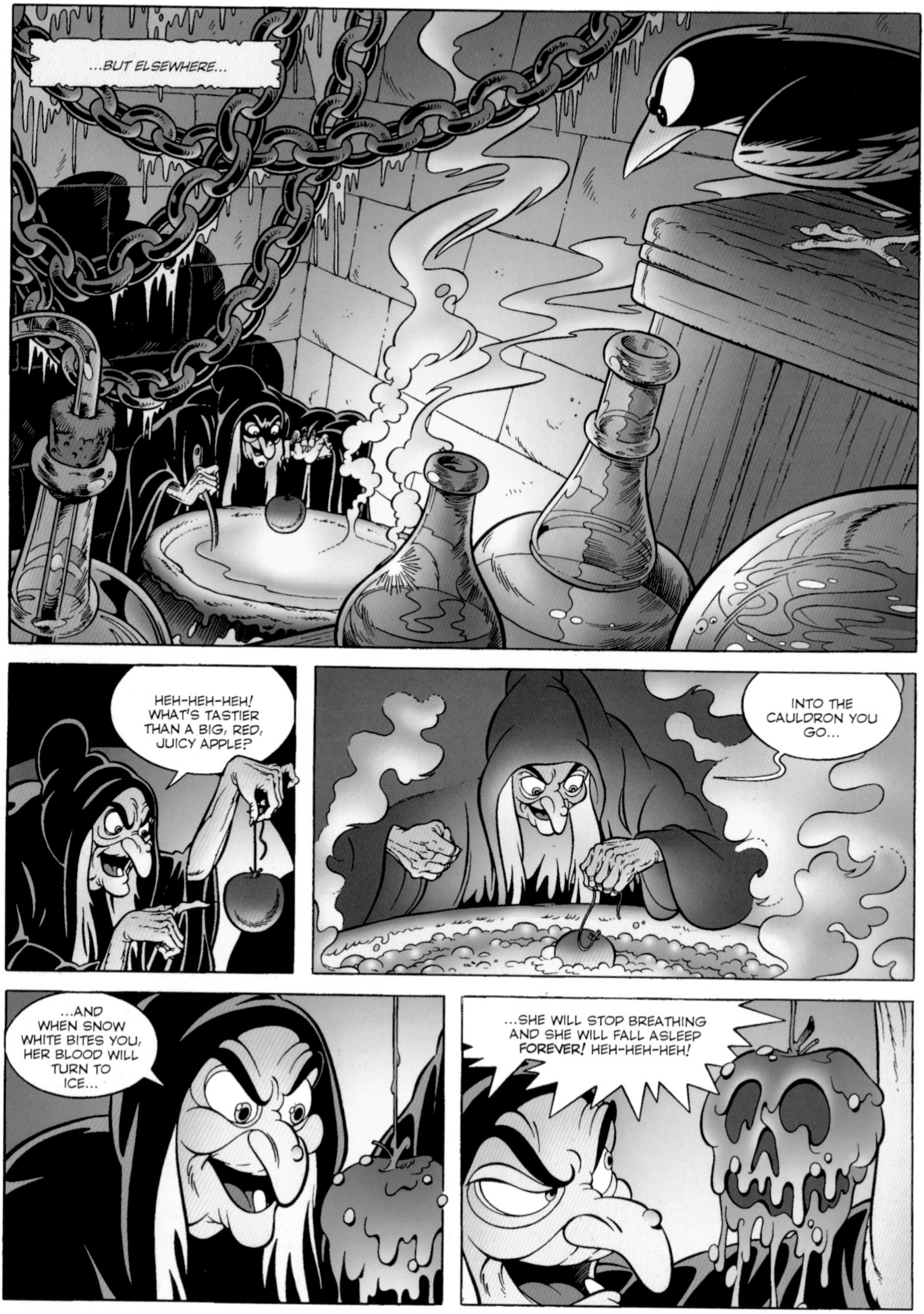
...BUT ELSEWHERE...
HEH-HEH-HEH! WHAT'S TASTIER THAN A BIG, RED, JUICY APPLE?
INTO THE CAULDRON YOU GO...
...AND WHEN SNOW WHITE BITES YOU, HER BLOOD WILL TURN TO ICE...
...SHE WILL STOP BREATHING AND SHE WILL FALL ASLEEP FOREVER! HEH-HEH-HEH!

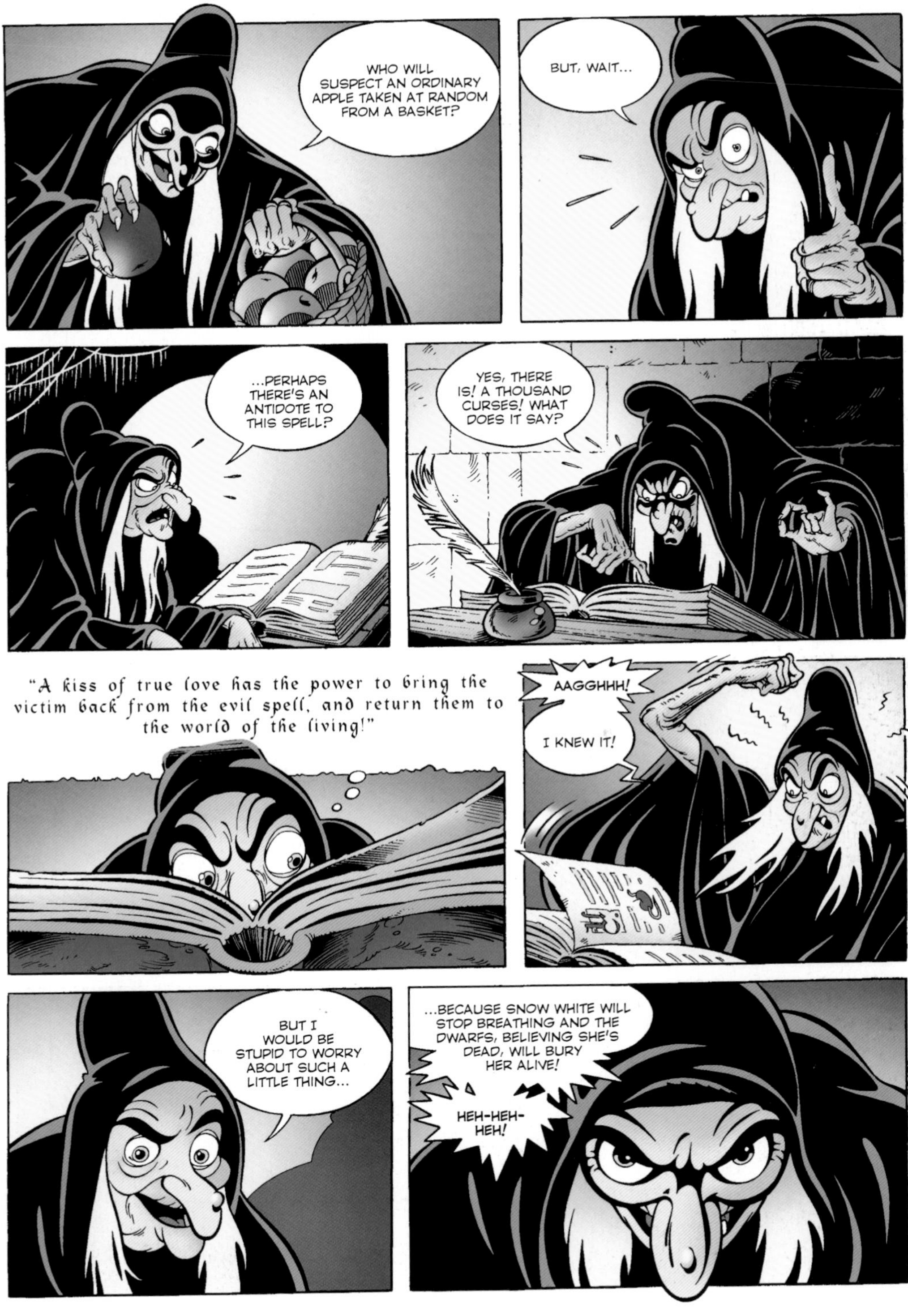
WHO WILL SUSPECT AN ORDINARY APPLE TAKEN AT RANDOM FROM A BASKET?
BUT, WAIT...
...PERHAPS THERE'S AN ANTIDOTE TO THIS SPELL?
YES, THERE IS! A THOUSAND CURSES! WHAT DOES IT SAY?
"A kiss of true love has the power to bring the victim back from the evil spell, and return them to the world of the living!"
AAGGHHH!
I KNEW IT!
BUT I WOULD BE STUPID TO WORRY ABOUT SUCH A LITTLE THING...
...BECAUSE SNOW WHITE WILL STOP BREATHING AND THE DWARFS, BELIEVING SHE'S DEAD, WILL BURY HER ALIVE!
HEH-HEH-HEH!

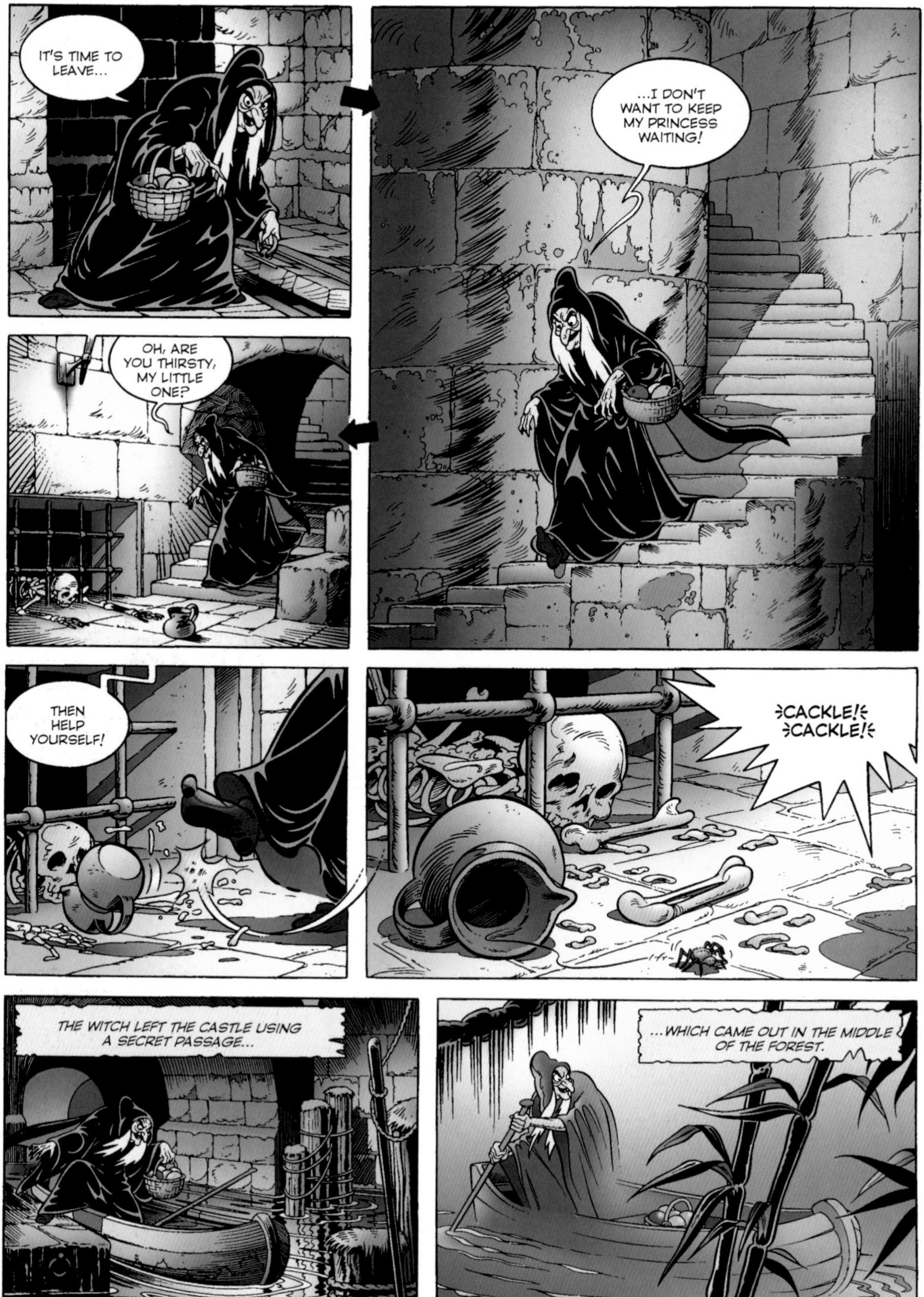
IT'S TIME TO LEAVE...
...I DON'T WANT TO KEEP MY PRINCESS WAITING!
OH, ARE YOU THIRSTY, MY LITTLE ONE?
THEN HELP YOURSELF!
CACKLE! CACKLE!
THE WITCH LEFT THE CASTLE USING A SECRET PASSAGE...
...WHICH CAME OUT IN THE MIDDLE OF THE FOREST.

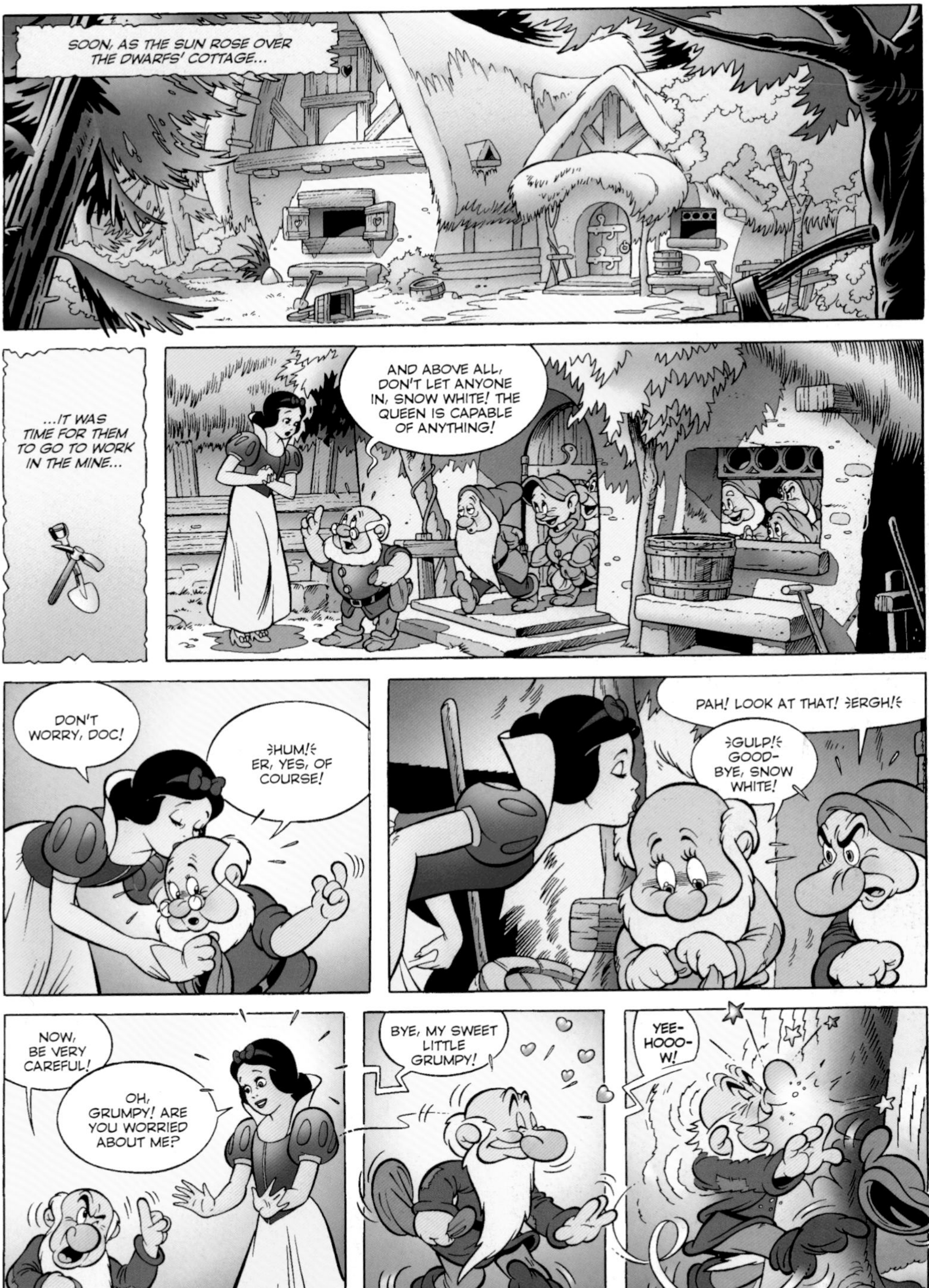
SOON, AS THE SUN ROSE OVER THE DWARFS' COTTAGE...
...IT WAS TIME FOR THEM TO GO TO WORK IN THE MINE...
AND ABOVE ALL, DON'T LET ANYONE IN, SNOW WHITE! THE QUEEN IS CAPABLE OF ANYTHING!
DON'T WORRY, DOC!
HUM! ER, YES, OF COURSE!
PAH! LOOK AT THAT! ERGH!
GULP! GOOD-BYE, SNOW WHITE!
NOW, BE VERY CAREFUL!
OH, GRUMPY! ARE YOU WORRIED ABOUT ME?
BYE, MY SWEET LITTLE GRUMPY!
YEE-HOOO-W!

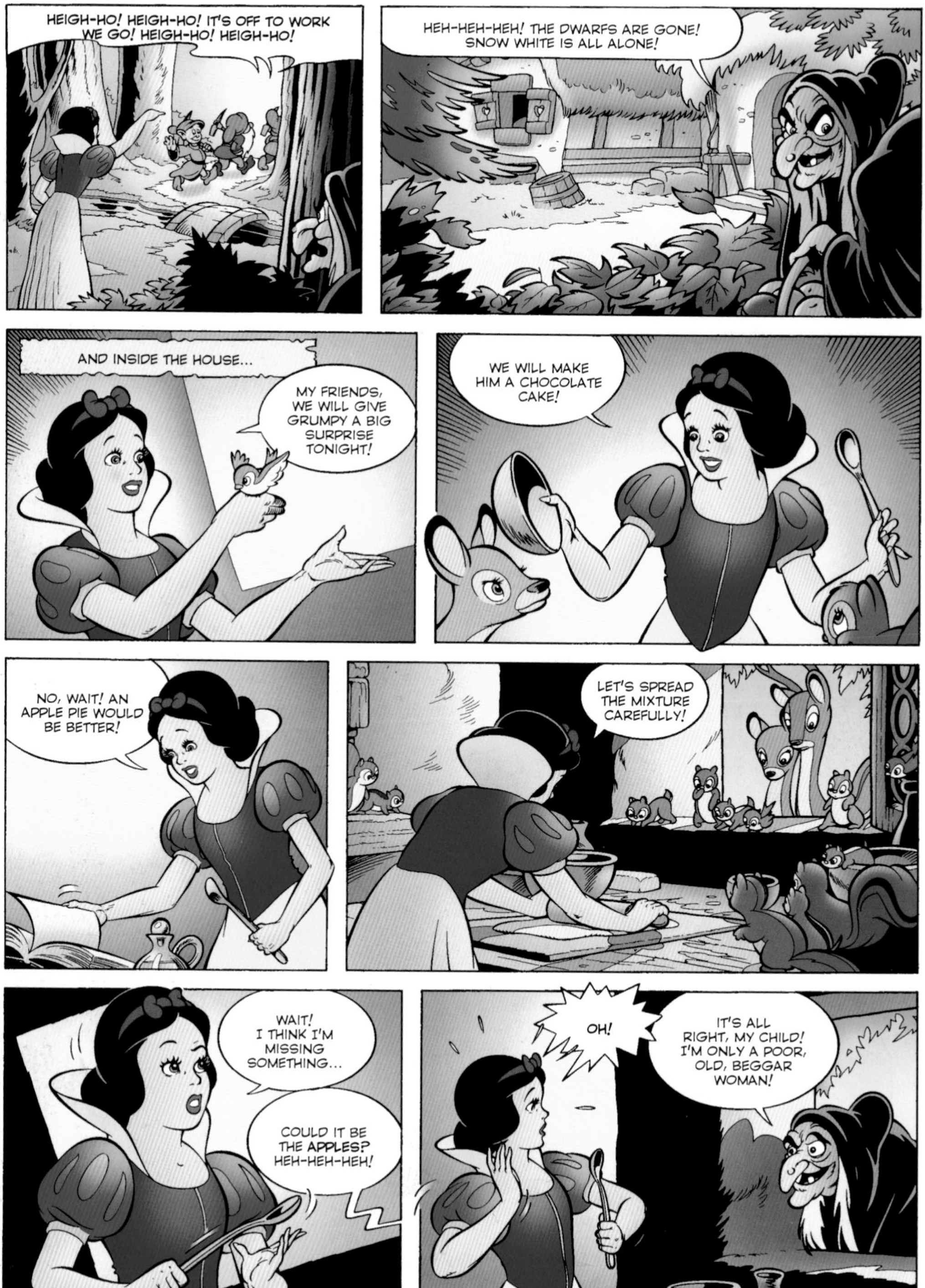

HEIGH-HO! HEIGH-HO! IT'S OFF TO WORK WE GO! HEIGH-HO! HEIGH-HO!
HEH-HEH-HEH! THE DWARFS ARE GONE! SNOW WHITE IS ALL ALONE!
AND INSIDE THE HOUSE...
MY FRIENDS, WE WILL GIVE GRUMPY A BIG SURPRISE TONIGHT!
WE WILL MAKE HIM A CHOCOLATE CAKE!
NO, WAIT! AN APPLE PIE WOULD BE BETTER!
LET'S SPREAD THE MIXTURE CAREFULLY!
WAIT! I THINK I'M MISSING SOMETHING...
COULD IT BE THE APPLES? HEH-HEH-HEH!
OH!
IT'S ALL RIGHT, MY CHILD! I'M ONLY A POOR, OLD, BEGGAR WOMAN!

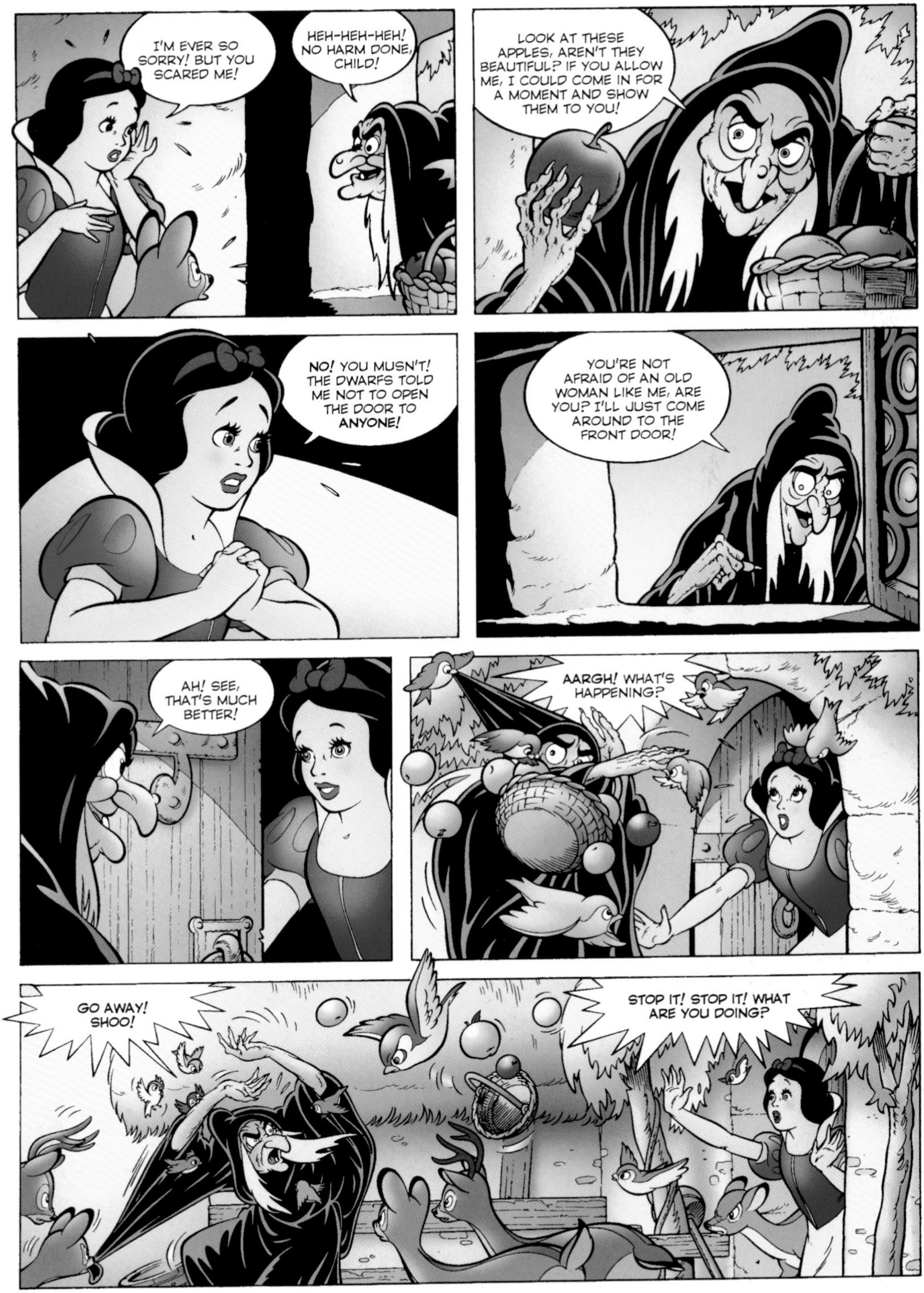
I'M EVER SO SORRY! BUT YOU SCARED ME!
HEH-HEH-HEH! NO HARM DONE, CHILD!
LOOK AT THESE APPLES, AREN'T THEY BEAUTIFUL? IF YOU ALLOW ME, I COULD COME IN FOR A MOMENT AND SHOW THEM TO YOU!
NO! YOU MUSN'T! THE DWARFS TOLD ME NOT TO OPEN THE DOOR TO ANYONE!
YOU'RE NOT AFRAID OF AN OLD WOMAN LIKE ME, ARE YOU? I'LL JUST COME AROUND TO THE FRONT DOOR!
AH! SEE, THAT'S MUCH BETTER!
AARGH! WHAT'S HAPPENING?
GO AWAY! SHOO!
STOP IT! STOP IT! WHAT ARE YOU DOING?

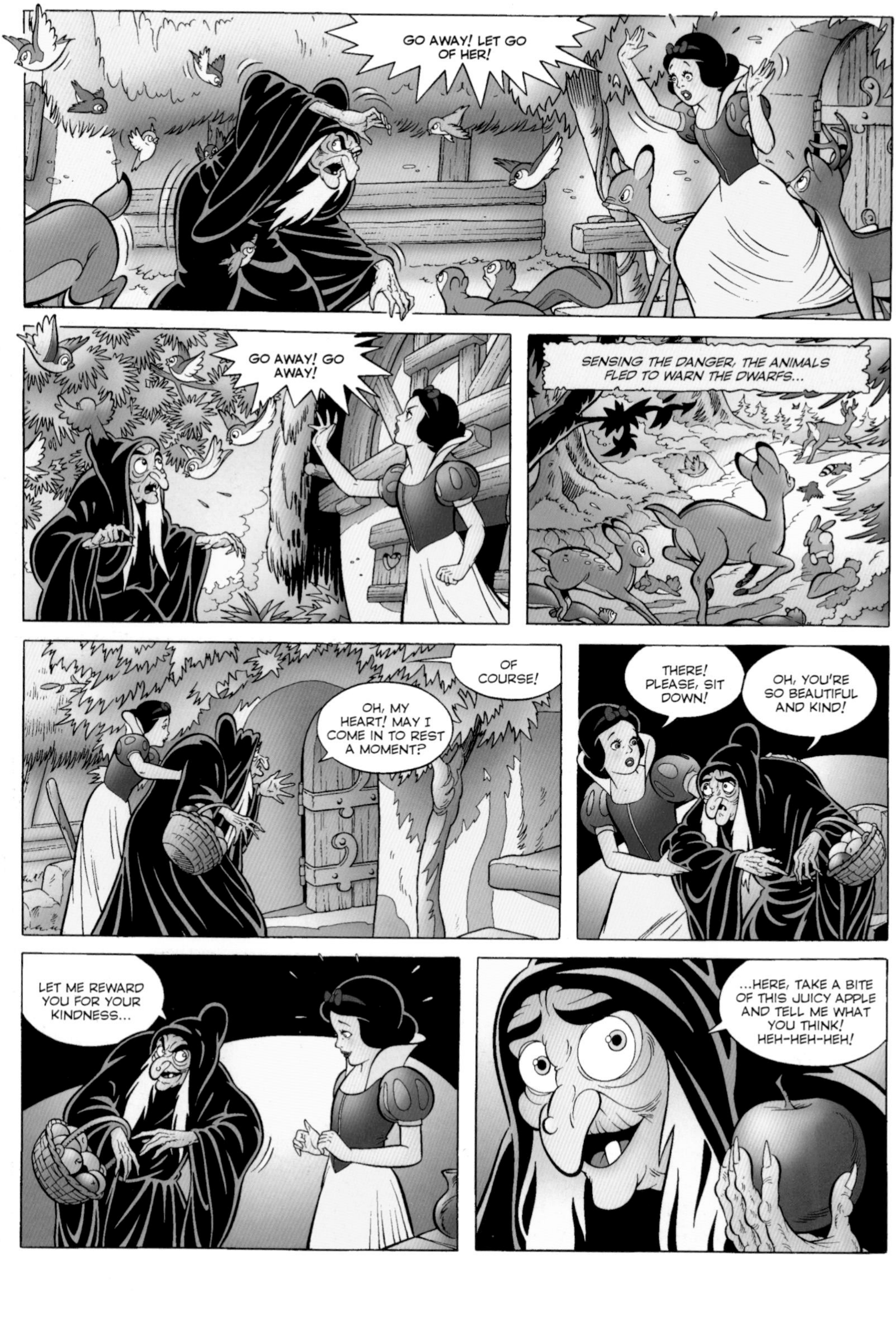
GO AWAY! LET GO OF HER!
GO AWAY! GO AWAY!
SENSING THE DANGER, THE ANIMALS FLED TO WARN THE DWARFS...
OH, MY HEART! MAY I COME IN TO REST A MOMENT?
OF COURSE!
THERE! PLEASE, SIT DOWN!
OH, YOU'RE SO BEAUTIFUL AND KIND!
LET ME REWARD YOU FOR YOUR KINDNESS...
...HERE, TAKE A BITE OF THIS JUICY APPLE AND TELL ME WHAT YOU THINK! HEH-HEH-HEH!

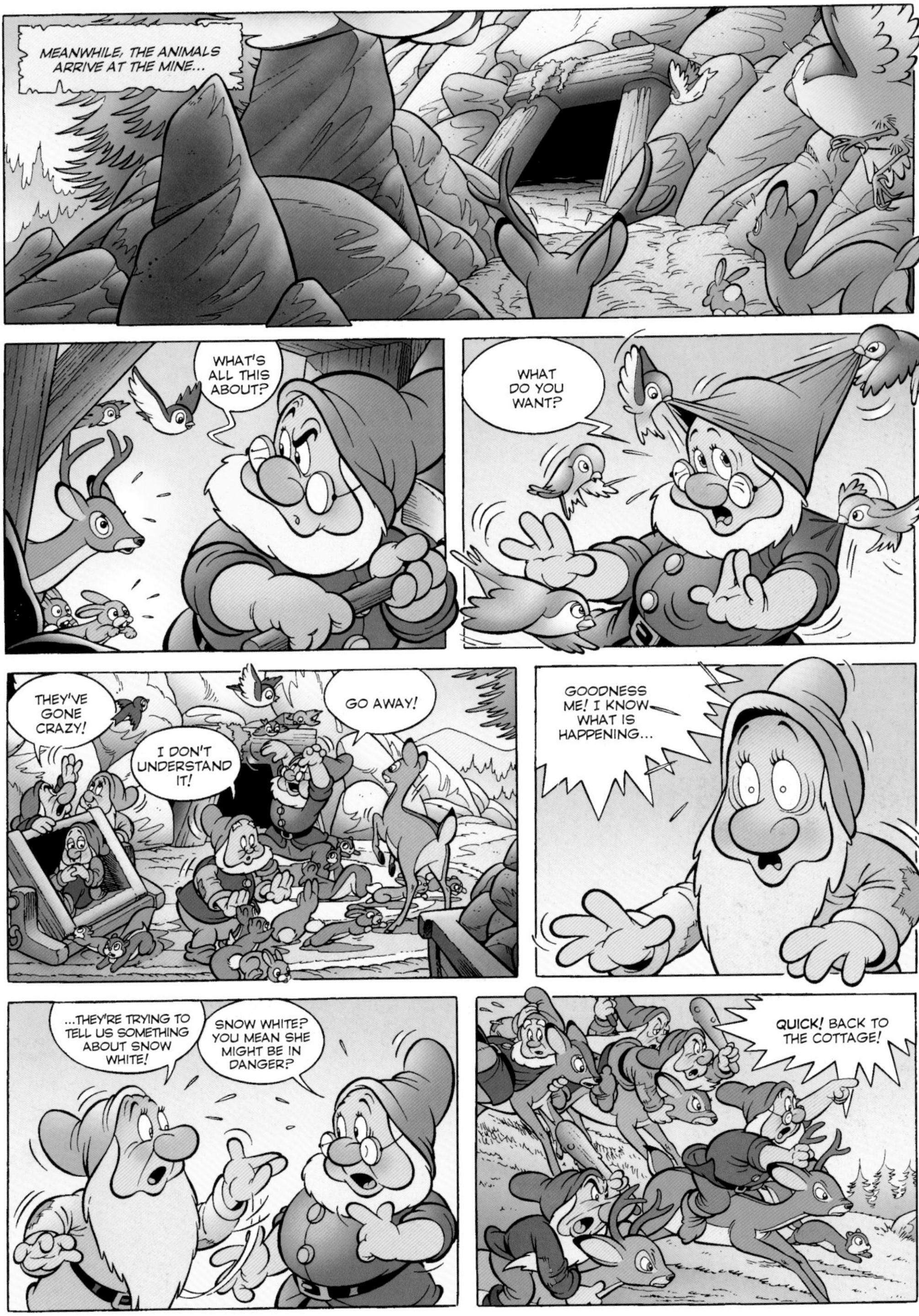
MEANWHILE, THE ANIMALS ARRIVE AT THE MINE...
WHAT'S ALL THIS ABOUT?
WHAT DO YOU WANT?
THEY'VE GONE CRAZY!
I DON'T UNDERSTAND IT!
GO AWAY!
GOODNESS ME! I KNOW WHAT IS HAPPENING...
...THEY'RE TRYING TO TELL US SOMETHING ABOUT SNOW WHITE!
SNOW WHITE? YOU MEAN SHE MIGHT BE IN DANGER?
QUICK! BACK TO THE COTTAGE!

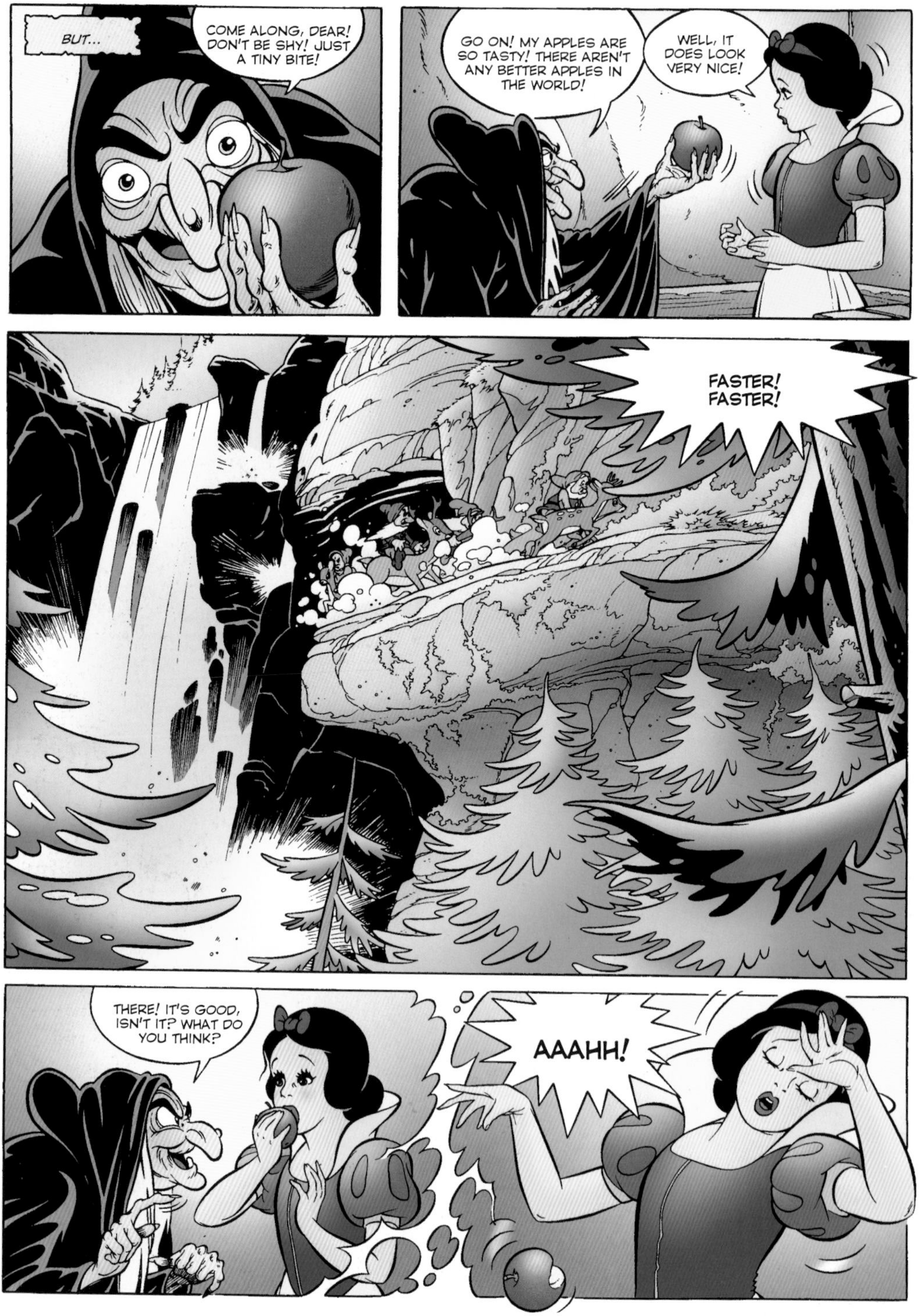

BUT...
COME ALONG, DEAR! DON'T BE SHY! JUST A TINY BITE!
GO ON! MY APPLES ARE SO TASTY! THERE AREN'T ANY BETTER APPLES IN THE WORLD!
WELL, IT DOES LOOK VERY NICE!
FASTER! FASTER!
THERE! IT'S GOOD, ISN'T IT? WHAT DO YOU THINK?
AAAHH!

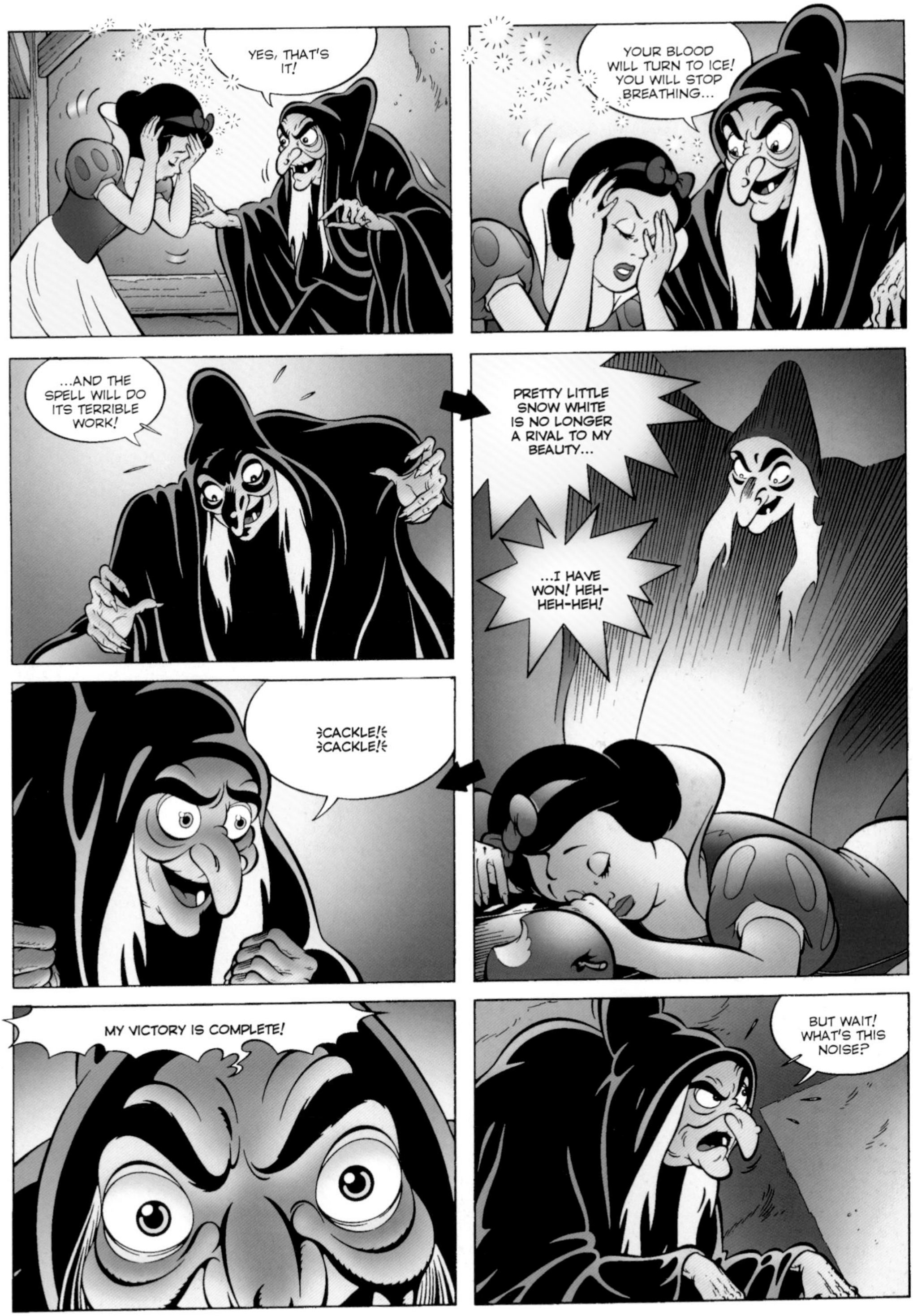
YES, THAT'S IT!
YOUR BLOOD WILL TURN TO ICE! YOU WILL STOP BREATHING...
...AND THE SPELL WILL DO ITS TERRIBLE WORK!
PRETTY LITTLE SNOW WHITE IS NO LONGER A RIVAL TO MY BEAUTY...
...I HAVE WON! HEH-HEH-HEH!
CACKLE! CACKLE!
MY VICTORY IS COMPLETE!
BUT WAIT! WHAT'S THIS NOISE?

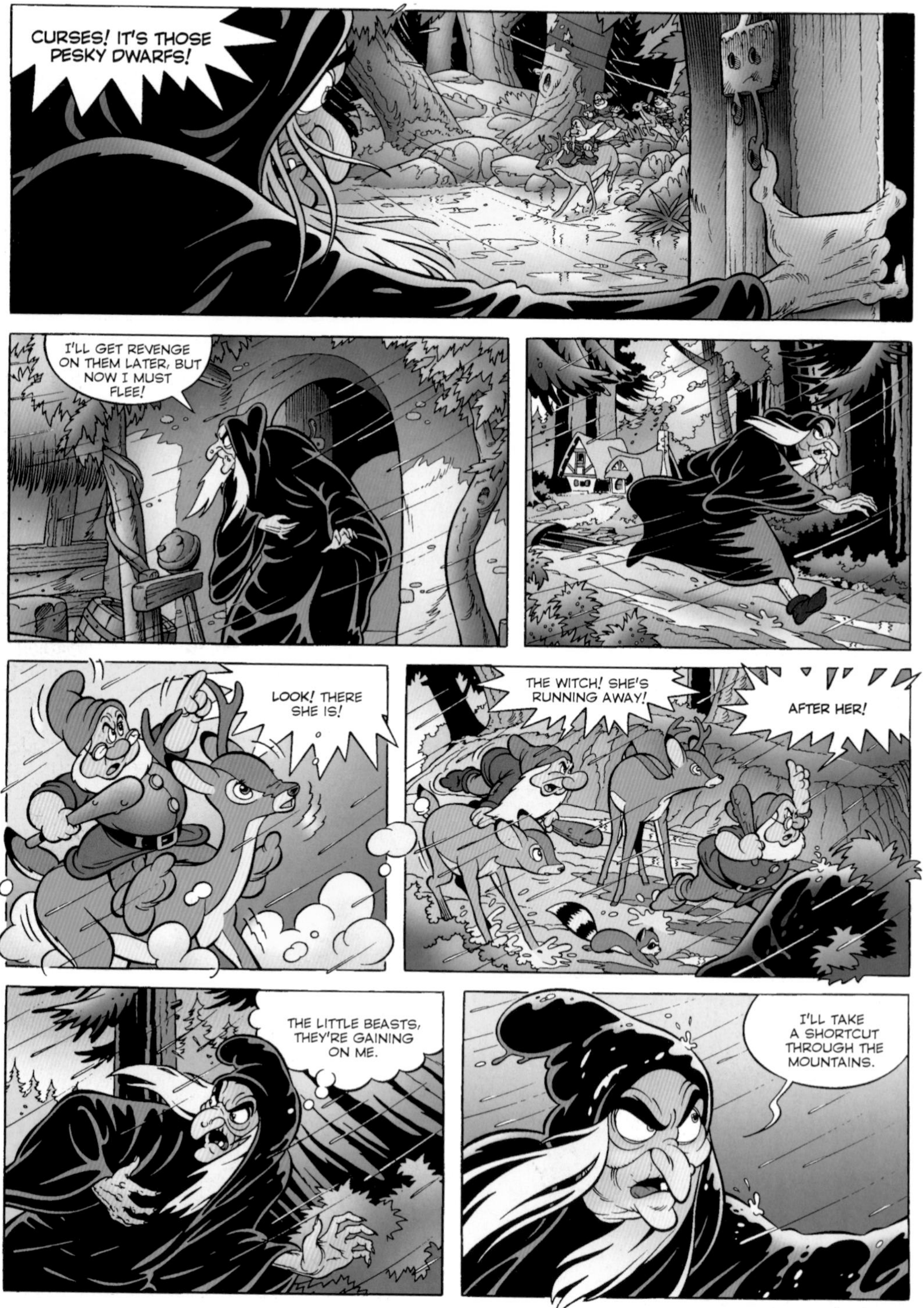
CURSES! IT'S THOSE PESKY DWARFS!
I'LL GET REVENGE ON THEM LATER, BUT NOW I MUST FLEE!
LOOK! THERE SHE IS!
THE WITCH! SHE'S RUNNING AWAY!
AFTER HER!
THE LITTLE BEASTS, THEY'RE GAINING ON ME.
I'LL TAKE A SHORTCUT THROUGH THE MOUNTAINS.

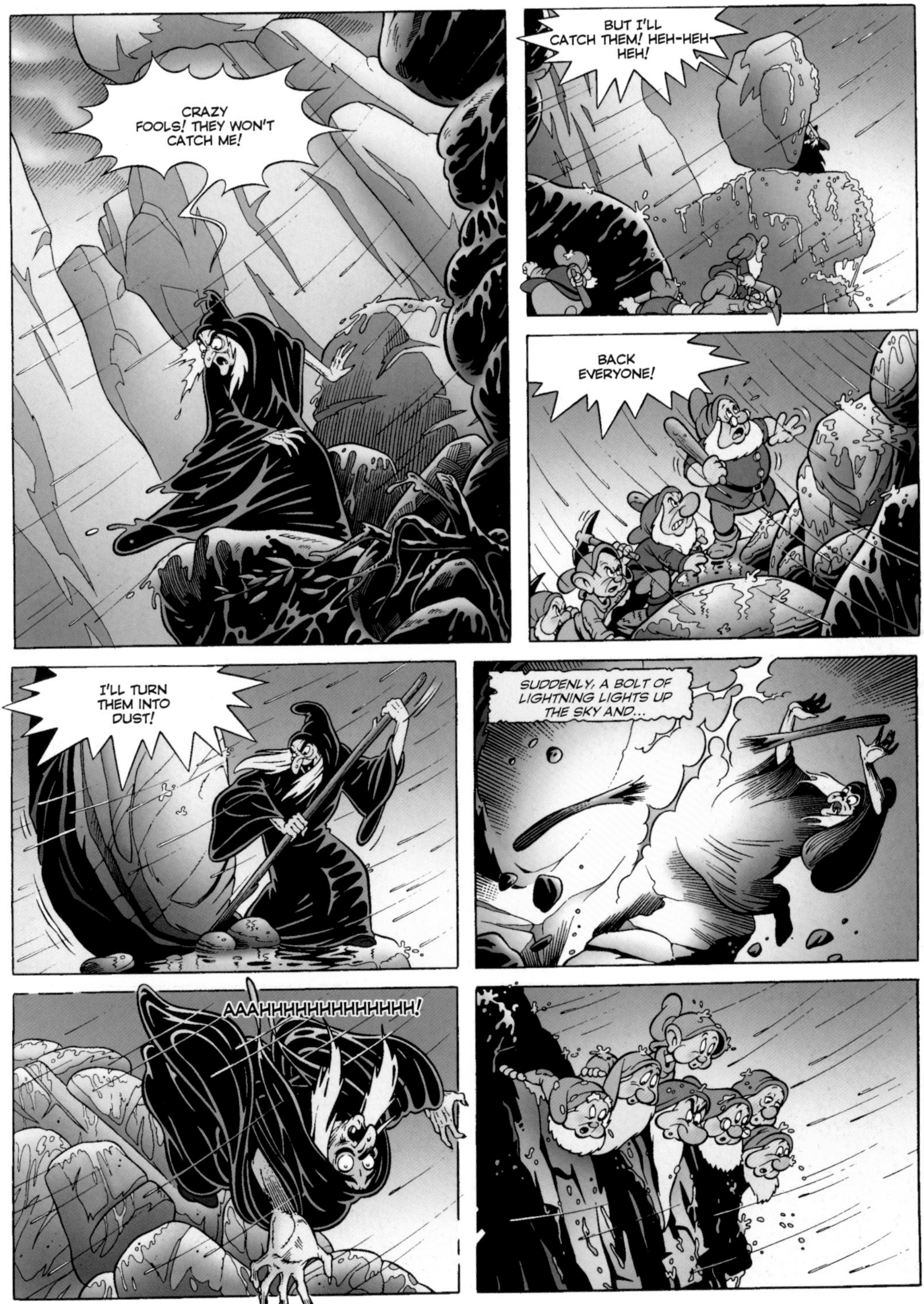
CRAZY FOOLS! THEY WON'T CATCH ME!
BUT I'LL CATCH THEM! HEH-HEH-HEH!
BACK EVERYONE!
I'LL TURN THEM INTO DUST!
SUDDENLY, A BOLT OF LIGHTNING LIGHTS UP THE SKY AND...
AAAHHHHHHHHHHHHH!

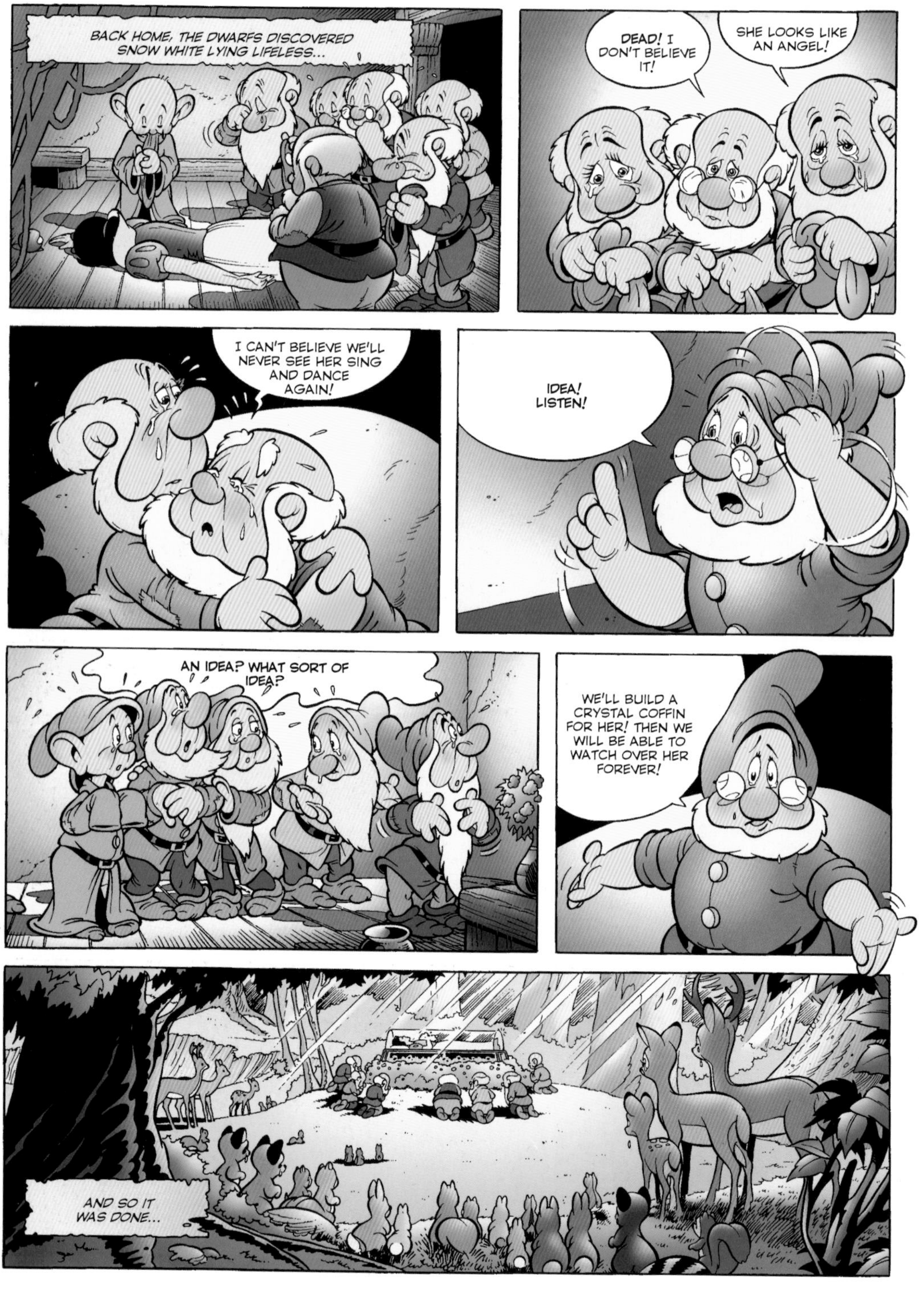
BACK HOME, THE DWARFS DISCOVERED SNOW WHITE LYING LIFELESS...
DEAD! I DON'T BELIEVE IT!
SHE LOOKS LIKE AN ANGEL!
I CAN'T BELIEVE WE'LL NEVER SEE HER SING AND DANCE AGAIN!
IDEA! LISTEN!
AN IDEA? WHAT SORT OF IDEA?
WE'LL BUILD A CRYSTAL COFFIN FOR HER! THEN WE WILL BE ABLE TO WATCH OVER HER FOREVER!
AND SO IT WAS DONE...

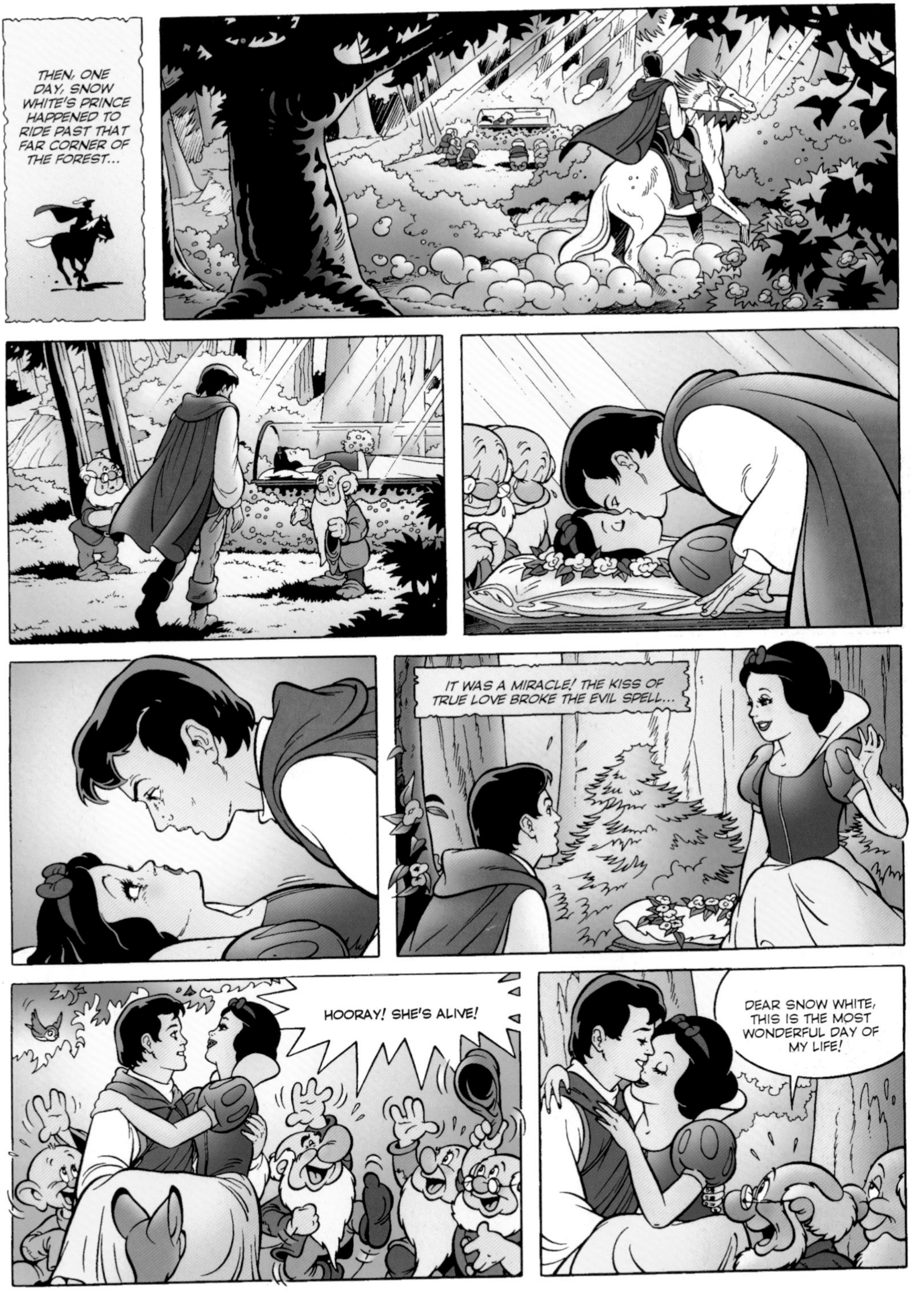
THEN, ONE DAY, SNOW WHITE'S PRINCE HAPPENED TO RIDE PAST THAT FAR CORNER OF THE FOREST...
IT WAS A MIRACLE! THE KISS OF TRUE LOVE BROKE THE EVIL SPELL...
HOORAY! SHE'S ALIVE!
DEAR SNOW WHITE, THIS IS THE MOST WONDERFUL DAY OF MY LIFE!

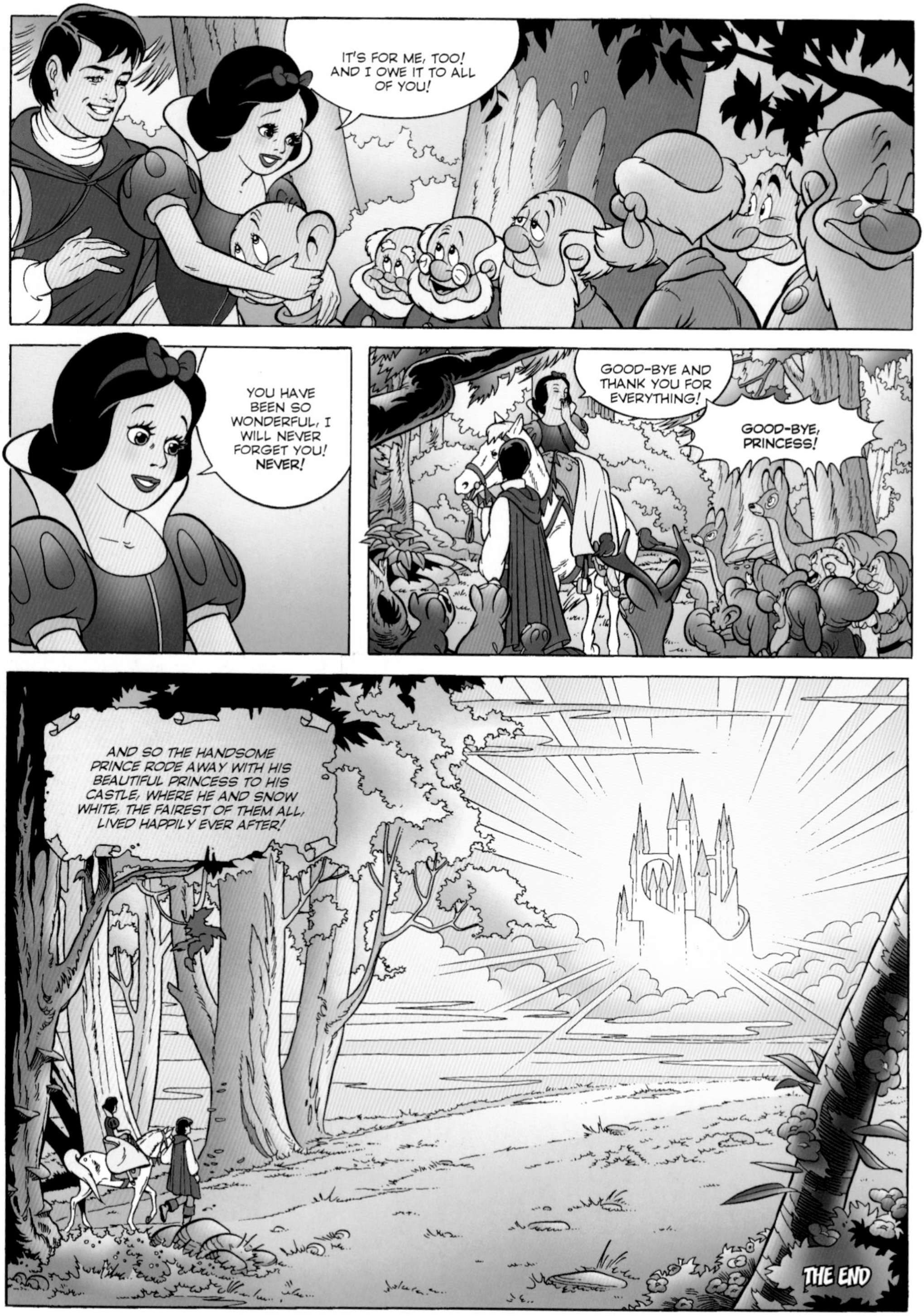
IT'S FOR ME, TOO! AND I OWE IT TO ALL OF YOU!
YOU HAVE BEEN SO WONDERFUL, I WILL NEVER FORGET YOU! NEVER!
GOOD-BYE AND THANK YOU FOR EVERYTHING!
GOOD-BYE, PRINCESS!
AND SO THE HANDSOME PRINCE RODE AWAY WITH HIS BEAUTIFUL PRINCESS TO HIS CASTLE, WHERE HE AND SNOW WHITE, THE FAIREST OF THEM ALL, LIVED HAPPILY EVER AFTER!
THE END

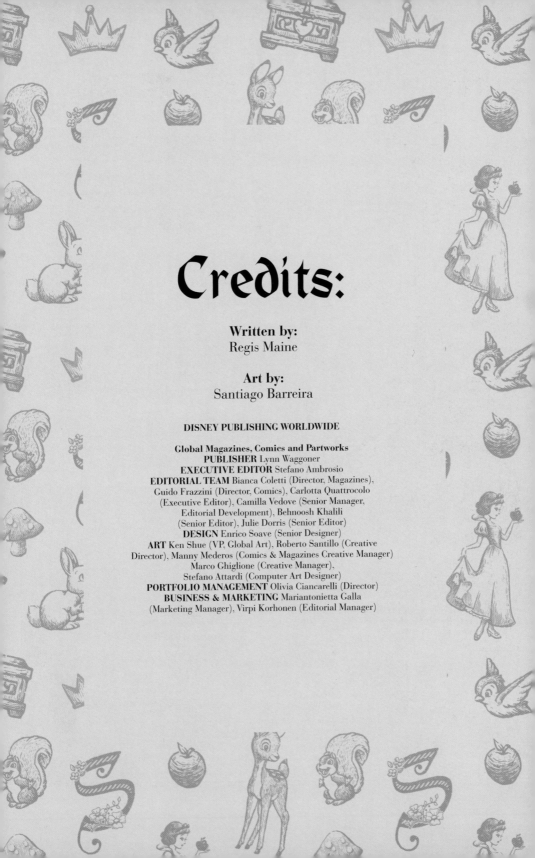

Credits:

Written by:
Regis Maine

Art by:
Santiago Barreira

DISNEY PUBLISHING WORLDWIDE

Global Magazines, Comics and Partworks
PUBLISHER Lynn Waggoner
EXECUTIVE EDITOR Stefano Ambrosio
EDITORIAL TEAM Bianca Coletti (Director, Magazines),
Guido Frazzini (Director, Comics), Carlotta Quattrocolo
(Executive Editor), Camilla Vedove (Senior Manager,
Editorial Development), Behnoosh Khalili
(Senior Editor), Julie Dorris (Senior Editor)
DESIGN Enrico Soave (Senior Designer)
ART Ken Shue (VP, Global Art), Roberto Santillo (Creative
Director), Manny Mederos (Comics & Magazines Creative Manager)
Marco Ghiglione (Creative Manager),
Stefano Attardi (Computer Art Designer)
PORTFOLIO MANAGEMENT Olivia Ciancarelli (Director)
BUSINESS & MARKETING Mariantonietta Galla
(Marketing Manager), Virpi Korhonen (Editorial Manager)

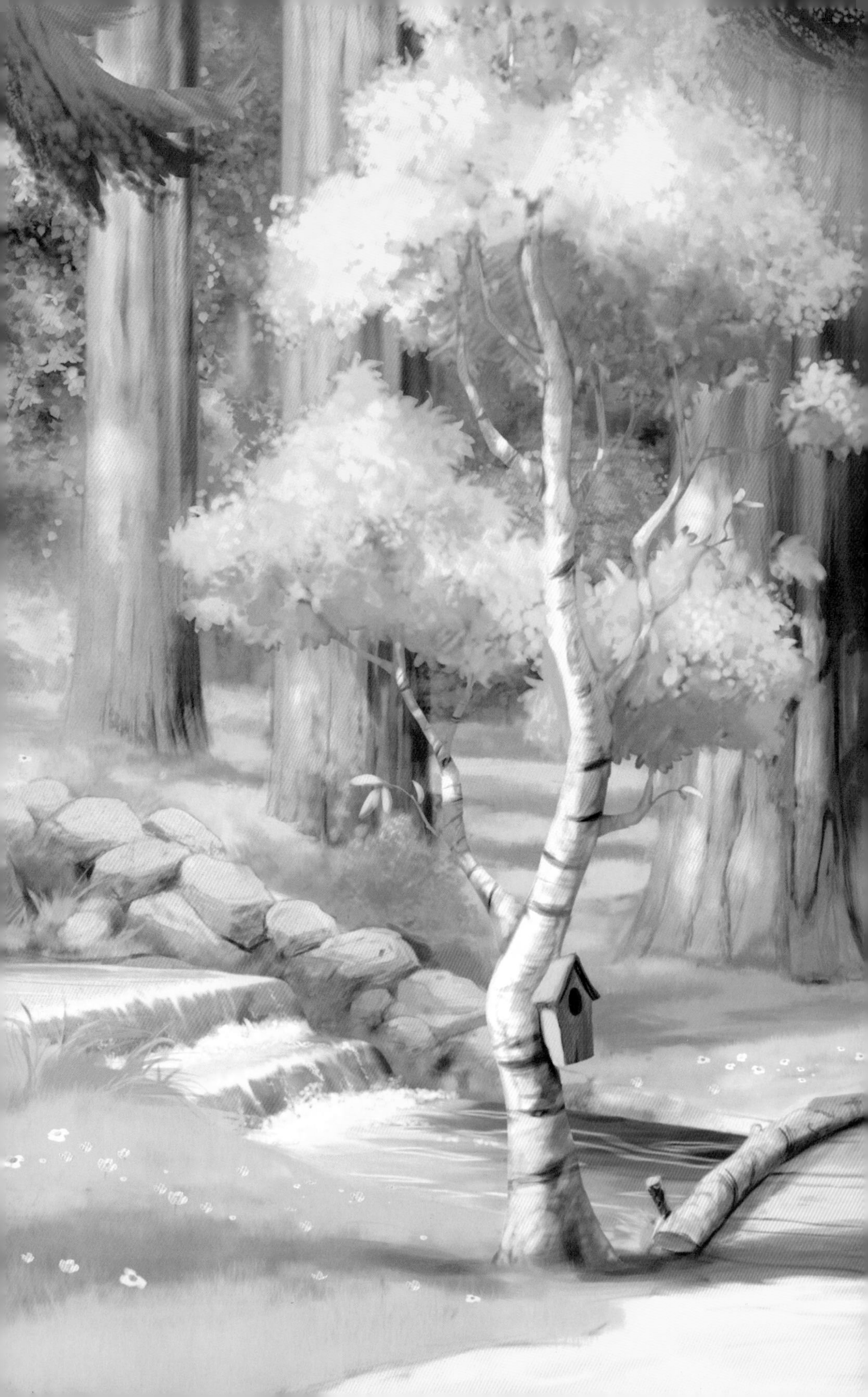

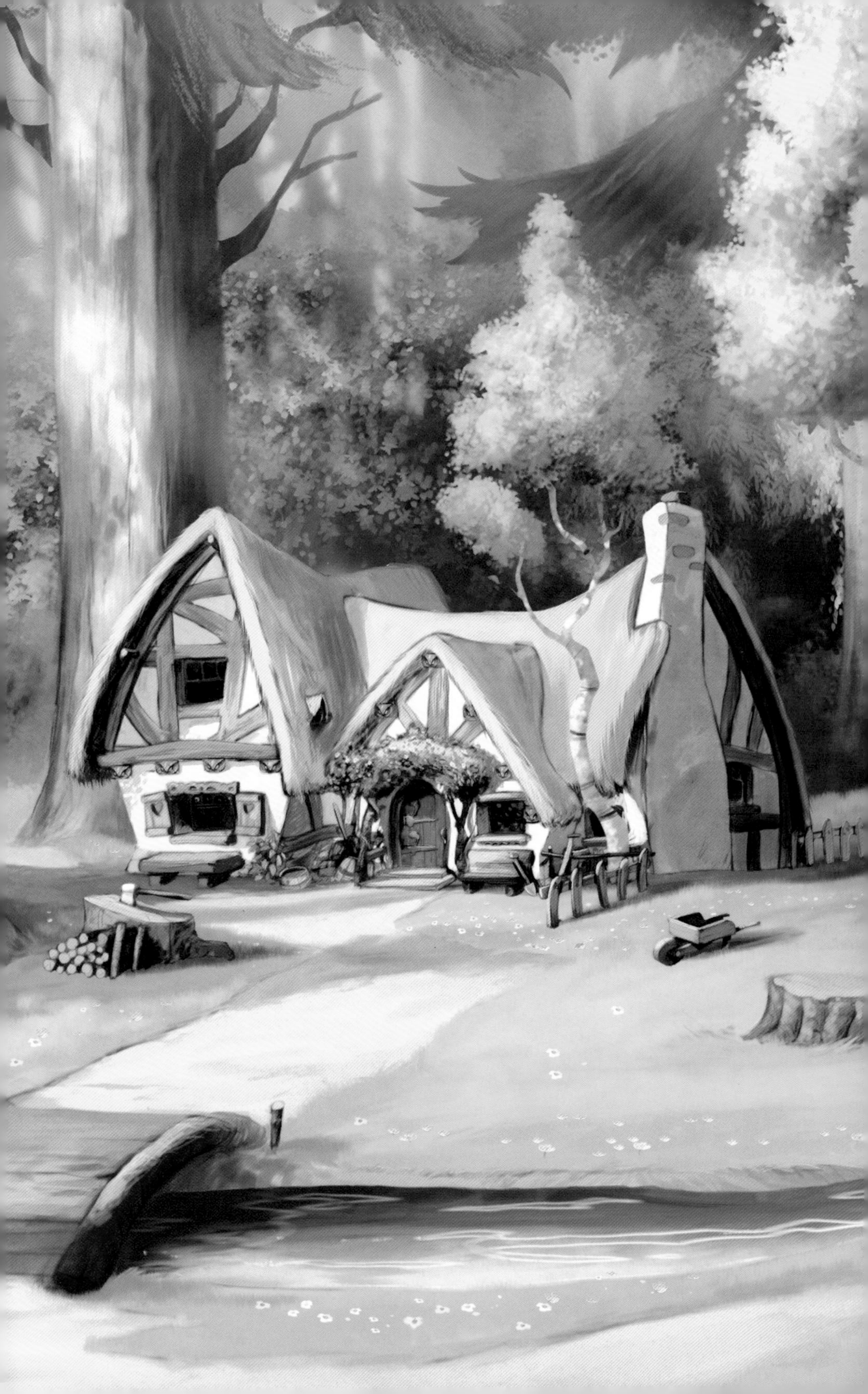

THE STORY OF THE MOVIE IN COMICS

THE STORY OF THE MOVIE IN COMICS
DISNEY
Tangled
DISNEY
COMICS

DISNEY

Tangled

DISNEY

THE LION KING

THE STORY OF THE MOVIE IN COMICS
DISNEY
THE LION KING
DISNEY
COMICS

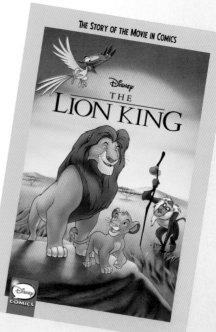